COLD EARTH WANDERERS

PETER WORTSMAN

Pelekinesis

PRAISE FOR PETER WORTSMAN

"The behavior of the people [in 'Snapshots and Souvenirs'] was wonderfully human and moving—the sort of thing even the best writers find it almost impossible to invent. The unexpected in human behavior is difficult to take out of the air, as opposed to the usual, which anyone can invent. So that it is precisely these unforeseen details which establish the authenticity of the text, and which give it its literary value... excellent."

–Paul Bowles, author of *The Sheltering Sky*

"*A Modern Way to Die* is a fantastic book and I thoroughly enjoyed it. I have never read anything quite like this, but my enjoyment was due to more than just novelty, it was a response to marvelous writing, wonderful craft, and the breath of imagination... [Wortsman] succeeded so well in his craft and art that it reads 'artless' and 'spontaneous,' which to me is the highest of compliments."

–Hubert Selby, Jr., author of *Last Exit to Brooklyn*

"Wortsman achieves a level of spontaneity and accessibility...to which most writers can only aspire."

–David Ulin, *The L.A. Weekly*

"Wortsman hangs with the masters."

–A. Scott Cardwell, *The Boston Phoenix*

"His work reminded me some of E.B. White's *New Yorker* stuff—observations turned into little reads but with a modernist twist."

–Ruth Lopez, *The New Mexican*

"Peter Wortsman, in the light of day, seems able to connect the power of the dream narrative to conscious language to create unique works that walk a curious line between fiction and poetry."

–Russell Edson, author of *The Tunnel: Selected Poems of Russell Edson*

OTHER BOOKS BY PETER WORTSMAN

A Modern Way to Die, Smallstories and Microtales,
  Fromm International Publishing Co., 1991

it - t = i, an artist's book, produced in collaboration
  with graphic artist, Harold Wortsman, here and
  now press, 2004

Ghost Dance in Berlin, A Rhapsody in Gray, Travelers'
  Tales, 2013

*Tales of the German Imagination: From the Brothers
  Grimm to Ingeborg Bachmann*, an anthology com-
  piled, edited and translated by Peter Wortsman,
  Penguin Classics, 2013

Brennende Worte, the German translation of the
  stage play *Burning Words*, by Peter Wortsman,
  translated from the English by Peter Torberg, Kul-
  turhaus Osterfeld, Pforzheim, Germany, 2014

Selected Translations:

Posthumous Papers of a Living Author, by Robert
  Musil, Volume One of Eridanos Library, Eridanos
  Press, 1988; second edition, Penguin 20th Cen-
  tury Classics, 1995; third edition, Archipelago
  Books, NYC, 2006; *Flypaper* (a selection from
  Posthumous Papers of a Living Author), Penguin
  Mini-Classics, Penguin Books, 2011

Peter Schlemiel, The Man Who Sold His Shadow, by Adelbert von Chamisso, Fromm International Publishing Co., 1993

Telegrams of the Soul, Selected Prose of Peter Altenberg, Archipelago Books, 2005

Selected Short Prose of Heinrich von Kleist, Archipelago Books, 2009

Selected Tales of the Brothers Grimm, Archipelago Books, 2013

The Creator, a fantasy, by Mynona (aka Salomo Friedlaender), Wakefield Press, 2014

Cold Earth Wanderers by Peter Wortsman

ISBN: 978-1-938349-17-1
eISBN: 978-1-938349-18-8
Library of Congress Control Number: 2013918332

Layout and Book Design by Mark Givens

Cover Design: Harold Wortsman

Cover image from a video by Anton Rey; originally reproduced on Man in the Elevator (Heiner Goebbels), ECM 1988.

Lower left cover image originally black and white by Mark Feldstein.

First Pelekinesis Printing 2014

www.pelekinesis.com

Cold Earth Wanderers

Peter Wortsman

To Claudie, Aurélie and Jacques, the warm bodies of my world

I travel'd thro' a Land of Men

A Land of Men & Women too

And heard & saw such dreadful things

As cold earth wanderers never knew...

William Blake
"The Mental Traveler"

I

1.

Like so many of the underage dreamers of his day, Elgin Marble had always longed to burrow outwards. He had heard that in the past great corridors ran north and south, east and west, that a few adjacent blocks called fields were left un-built, and that entire freestanding zones called forests were unencumbered by human habitation. Contemporary life was unremittingly vertical.

Then came the dreaded knock.

–"It's time, Mr. Marble!"

"Run, Daddy, run!" Elgin pleaded, but to no avail, for the elevator operators, the EOs, were always quick about their business, breaking down the door, if need be, strapping the reluctant statistic down on the stretcher for the chloroforming—an unnecessary precaution in the case of Mr. Marble, an upstanding citizen and himself a recently retired EO, prepared to do his duty—and in any case there was nowhere to run to.

The day they dragged his dad off to the occupant disposal chute, the ODC as it was commonly called, perfumed, drugged, laid out and draped with a plastic wreath and the requisite salutation: One for the Good of All, with family and friends dutifully marching behind, his tear ducts cried dry, Elgin knew he wanted out.

*

"Work hard," his mother told him, "and maybe you'll grow up to be a fine EO like your father!"

Elgin nodded.

Ellen Marble, who understood her son all too well and could read the unspoken flutter of his lip, looked around, ever fearful of the electric ears and eyes in the walls and the bugs which, it was said by some, were implanted in the soft stuffing of pillows to read your dreams.

As a child, Elgin had pieced together a model train from tin cans with punctured holes and twisted clips for wheels. Accustomed to camouflaging her son's inclination, Ellen had to hold the train aloft from engine to caboose when neighbors' kids dropped by, dubbing his creation a five-car commuter elevator.

Mrs. Marble laughed uncomfortably: "My boy has such a vivid vertical imagination!"

2.

Like everyone else, the Marbles were assigned a block to which their motion was restricted from birth to disposal.

Each block was a world unto itself, with residential cubes, school sectors, businesses, and leisure tubes all stacked one on top of another, that rose many miles into the sky, with its foundation and sub-sub basement space embedded deep in the bedrock below. Furthermore, for the privileged few, every block had its assigned segment of planetary resort zone reached by rocket from the rooftop launch pad, and its trade route with "China," or more precisely, the blocks whose basement levels bordered on their own.

Teachers were trained to detect any horizontal leanings in delinquent dreamers. Nevertheless, try as they might, the Institute for Vertical Thinking (IVT) failed, despite endless experimentation, to cleanse the mind of illicit longings.

The unmarked horizon parlors located in certain designated shafts, where the higher-ups mixed business and pleasure, doubled, unbeknownst even to their privileged patrons, as psychosocial laboratories where IVT operatives tested the effects of horizontal simulation tubes on virtual travelers. Patrons selected a destination on the panel: California, Calcutta, Qatar and other fabled locales, and a hostess would emerge, appropriately attired in bikini, sari or burka, beckoning the "passenger" into a simulated sleeping car, complete with comfort station and bar.

"All aboard!" cried a canned conductor, followed by the sound of hissing steam and the simulated cries of leave-takers milling about on the virtual platform: "Bon voyage!" "Don't forget to write!" "Tell Mother I'll be home for Christmas!"

The simulated journey that followed took the virtual traveler on a historical jaunt, in the course of which his trained hostess pointed out all the sites and statistics, population density, production level, etc.

"Want to get horizontal?" she would suggest with a programmed smile precisely ten minutes into the trip, whereupon she pulled the seat out into a double palette. A wall panel (one-way window from the far side) enabled the traveler to take in the scenery screened for his viewing pleasure while he was otherwise engaged, and simultaneously permitted the IVT to study the response, with additional agents assigned to monitor the agent on duty for horizontal reverberations.

3.

Befitting her status as the widowed wife of an EO, Mrs. Marble grew African violets and orchids in her leisure cube.

"Your violets, Ellen, are just divine!" remarked her neighbor, Gladys Loyola with a certain unabashed envy. The two women maintained a cordial commodity exchanging relationship. Mrs. Loyola, the wife of an elevator supervisor (ES) officiated as the IVT Ladies Auxiliary floor chairlady, and so it was important to stay in her good graces.

–"It's all a matter of carefully calibrated artificial light setting and nitrates, Gladys!"

–"I try, Ellen dear, but my orchids always wilt!"

–"Maybe you over-stimulate them with plant growth products. Orchids are very sensitive, you know."

–"Oh, Ellen, you really must teach me sensitivity one day. It's the one subject I didn't do well on in training. Herbert, Sr. thinks it's dangerous to feel too much."

–" I wouldn't worry, Gladys!"

–"Speaking of which, Ellen, I've been meaning to tell you, Elgin has been acting oddly."

–"Oddly?"

–"Herbert, Jr. tells me Elgin won't play 3-D chess with him any more."

–"Really!?"

–"Herbert, Jr. checkmated him last Sunday when he wasn't paying attention."

–"Did he?"

–"Yes, and Elgin got so mad he pinned poor Herbert, Jr. down and stuffed the queen into his mouth."

–"That's terrible, Gladys! I'll be sure to talk to the boy when he gets home from school."

–"I'd watch him carefully if I were you, Ellen. He

has been acting strangely since his father's lovely disposal. Wouldn't want him to visit the 13th Floor!"

Most tenants of Block 367790 had never set foot on the 13th Floor and never hoped to. The passenger elevator bypassed that floor as if it didn't exist, but everyone trembled as they rose from 12 to 14, and though the walls were supposed to muffle unpleasant noises, an occasional reverberating cry pierced the reinforced concrete shell and echoed in the elevator shaft as the car whizzed by. Some said it was canned and deliberately planted in the PA system to set off the appropriate tremors. "The wheels need oiling!" the EO smiled uncomfortably.

4.

A week after Mr. Marble's disposal, on his way to school Elgin spotted a man stretched out in an out-of-order freight elevator.

"Where am I?" asked the rumpled derelict, rubbing his eyes.

"What a disgrace!" sneered a disapproving female block marshal who snuck up behind and prodded the sluggard with a spark from her joystick. Patched on the derelict's dirty shirtsleeve, the incensed BM spotted and read aloud the number 367789. "You don't belong here, buster!"

Before then, Elgin had never met anyone numbered anything but 367790, like himself. Elgin stared hard, wanting to take in the stranger's every feature and physical attribute. In school, they were taught that people from other blocks looked different, but aside from the man's disheveled clothes and the fact that he was badly in need of a bath, he looked pretty much like everyone else.

"Stand back, son!" the BM ordered.

But Elgin didn't budge.

"Get lost!" the officer yelled, menacingly waving her joystick.

Running down the hallway, the sound of shouting made Elgin look back. The derelict had broken loose and was running too. But all of the emergency stairway exits were locked for the police action. The only open door was the one leading to the ODC.

"Quick, in here!" Elgin motioned the fugitive into his family cube. His mother wasn't home. The boot steps of the BM clip-clopped down the hallway.

"You're taking an awful risk, son!" said the man from Block 367789, rubbing his gut where the officer had pronged him.

"So are you!" said Elgin, staring at the stranger with open-mouthed awe, barely able to get the syllables out of his mouth. "What's it like in Block 367789?"

"Pretty much the same as here," the man shrugged.

"How 'bout a bandage for that bruise," Elgin offered, "and a zapped cup of soup?"

The man shrugged again.

But the boy was as good as his word.

As the man wrapped the bandage around his middle and snapped the easy-open lid off the steaming cup, sipping his soup, he cracked a smile. "Better watch that curiosity, kid! Only place it'll get you is the 13th floor."

–"There's one in your block too?"

–"There's a 13th floor in every block."

–"How do you know?"

–"Let's just say I have it on good authority."

–"What's it like?"

–"You're asking too many questions for your own good, kid!"

–"What did they charge you with?"

–"Elevator banditry."

–"Did you do it?"

–"Of course I did, just like everyone else! My only problem was I brought back a can of sardines for my kids. The supervisor wanted it for himself. I refused. 'I can make things difficult for you,' he warned. 'Listen,' I said, 'my son has never tasted a sardine.' So they booked me and the son of a bitch took the sardines!"

–"What's it like?"

–"Like a sardine can!"

–"Seriously!"

–"Seriously!" the man slurped his soup.

The BM's boot steps were once again audible in the corridor.

"She's backtracking!" the man from Block 367789 observed. "I'll give those boots a few seconds to fade and then I'd best be on my way."

"But where will you go?" Elgin worried.

"Why such concern?!" the man grew suspicious. "Your old man isn't IVT, is he!?"

–"They shafted Daddy with honors last week!"

–"Sorry, son!" The man shook his head. "Listen, I haven't got much time. You ever heard of the Crabs?"

–"In Second Grade, Miss Alpine used to warn us if we turned our sheet of paper the wrong way: 'The Crabs'll come and get you!' I always imagined them as horrible defective robots with pincers that snapped your spine and crushed your skull."

The man flashed a fleeting smile. "That's what

they want you to believe. There are tunnels, you know!"

–"I saw a segment once on Inter-Eye. The IVT detected and demolished the last of them eons ago."

--Quick as they destroy 'em, we dig 'em, lead-lined with anti-detection devices! The IVT plants informants, desperate men who don't want to do another stint on the 13th floor. Can't blame 'em, the poor devils. That's the only way the authorities ever detect a new tunnel." The man put his ear to the door. "Coast clear, I'd best be off!"

"Good luck!" Elgin whispered.

"Thanks, kid!" the man reached for the door knob, then turned back to Elgin.—"I'm gonna tell you a secret," he whispered, "there are mind tunnels too!"

5.

In the months following her husband's disposal, Mrs. Marble was unable to control the boy. Elgin ran with a reckless crowd dedicated to committing horizontal pranks.

"Elgin," she pleaded, "for heaven's sake, think of your future! At the rate you're going, you'll never be a dog catcher, let alone make EO!"

"I love you, Mom," Elgin smiled, and unlike his

desensitized peers, gave her a hug and a kiss every morning on his way to school.

"Be careful!" his mother cautioned, secretly pleased. For Mrs. Marble was proud of her son. No one could fault him on his school performance. The boy got consistently high grades on his report-cues, generally accompanied by a blinking Code 7 IOA (Internally Over Active) warning. She smiled to herself, knowing full well that she was at least in part responsible for this dangerous propensity in her son. Elgin was her only child, and she had always had a powerful influence on him—until now, that is, when his willful ways took on a life of their own.

She had never, in fact, concerned herself with Elgin's academic performance—"I'm spoiled!" she'd always boasted with a smile to Gladys Loyola—until she received an electronic notification (EN) and the order to appear in person at the principal's office, instead of the customary bi-monthly parent-teacher exchange.

"Has Elgin done anything wrong?!" she immediately burst out at the principal's door.

Dr. Orion peered severely over the rim of his glasses blocked from a precipitous downwards slide by the bridge of his nose and passed an oily right palm over his bald pate. He did not rise to meet her or extend a hand of greeting. "Be seated, Mrs.

Marble!"

"But his report-cues have been practically perfect!" she protested in advance of any as yet unspoken charges.

"*Practically!*" he allowed.

–"Have there been too many latenesses?"

"Negative," replied Dr. Orion, maintaining the same deadpan expression. His candor was a highly prized quality at the Block Board of Education, that and his low sensitivity rating, qualities that helped him rise in the administrative ranks.

"Elgin hasn't been himself of late, the boy was unusually affected by his father's...*departure*," she said, making sure to employ the proper euphemism.

"I see," said Dr. Orion.

"Coming as it did, regrettably at the very onset of his peak period of hormonal hyperactivity"—she opted for the preferred term, eschewing the outdated word, adolescence—"you can well understand how missing his father might upset him as it does."

"Regrettable," observed Dr. Orion. Reaching into the middle drawer of his shining stainless steel desk, he pulled out a standard examination disk, slipped it into his computer and turned the screen toward her. "Do have a look!"

Staring at the screen, Mrs. Marble read her son's name and the misspelled word *compostition*.—"His spelling was never perfect!" She flashed a nervous smile.

"It isn't the spelling, Mrs. Marble, it's the contents. Consider his response to the suggested proposition: *There's nowhere to go but up!* on his block citizenship school composition. Read it!"

"I will," she assured him, but when she reached across the desk to press the eject button on the computer to retrieve the composition disk, Mr. Orion's gaze sharpened.

"Now!" he said.

And she read:

Scandalized by the sight of naked steps going nowhere, the grownups deny the enigma of a solitary flight into the void. They want their stairways suitably dressed and sandwiched in between floors, lest they forget which foot goes next and fall. But kids take things in stride. Daredevils dash up the twenty or so steps and leap off the landing. The more timid ones merely imagine the jump. The daredevils taunt the timid. The timid run home crying. In the safety of familiar stairwells, angels in training, they practice imaginary leaps.

"It's brief," Mrs. Marble allowed, trying to glean from the principal's expressionless gaze if this was its primary fault.

–"It isn't the length, Mrs. Marble, it's the implied proposition."

"Oh yes, of course," she replied, still puzzled.

"The underlying attitude," he reiterated.

"There are no latent horizontal tendencies, as far as I can tell!" she came back on the defensive, careful to employ the proper terminology.

–"It's retrograde, Mrs. Marble, positively retrograde!"

–"But climbing stairs is, after all, still good for the heart, is it not?"

–"Come, come, Madam, there are treadmills and stair simulators for that!"

–"Yes, but surely it's an innocent lapse!"

"Retrograde thought!" the principal pedantically corrected, shoving his glasses up the oily bridge of his nose with barely repressed rage. "As the boy's mother, you need to know that I've had a copy forwarded to the IVT Psychosocial Lab." The principal skillfully employed pauses for their intimidating effect. "Thank you for coming. That will be all."

6.

Mrs. Marble rode the elevator home in a daze. Where had she gone wrong? If only Upton were here to talk some sense into the boy. Memory banks would have to do.

Responsibly, as soon as he'd received the disposal notice, Upton Marble had gotten to work preparing his departure tapes and happy home holograms. He knew how important it would be for his son to preserve a vivid image of him once he was gone, and how important it would be for his wife too.

First off, of course, there were the official testament tapes. The language was prescribed:

Being of sound mind and body, I, Upton Marble, Elevator Operator in good standing, Block 367790, gladly restore to the block the nutritive and hydro rations assigned to me at birth, as well as the bonus allotments. May the block be vertical to my wife, Ellen, and son, Elgin, and permit them to retain a just portion of said allotment in accordance with their minimum basic needs...etc. etc.

The preparation of private departure tapes of a more personal nature, though frowned upon, was, nevertheless, tolerated by law. Acceptable parameters were recommended.

"Son," Mr. Marble began on the tape he prepared for Elgin, to go along with the standing manly *Hug Me!* hologram of himself, "the most potent antidote to depression is determination. You may get gloomy from time to time, but when you do, don't give in! Your mother and I decided not to have you desensitized, a fact which will make life much more difficult for you, but also, we believe, more rewarding, etc…"

But Ellen Marble reached for the *Conjugal Farewell*:

"My darling," Mr. Marble whispered again and again, his presence simulated by the reclining romantic *Hold Me!* hologram of her husband, which Ellen switched on every night, and in the implied arms of which she lay, trying to pretend intimacy. The sound and sight of him was soothing as she wept quietly, night after night, careful that Elgin not notice. If only Upton had input a responsive capacity and the software for virtual dialogue and contact with the departed, but there was no time, she thought, wiping the tears.

*

Now that biomedical advances had made disease more or less obsolete and had genetically engineered virtual immortality, the outdated notion of "natural death" was relegated to etymological dictionaries, though such colloquial expressions as "dead end," "dead weight" and "dead right" were still employed by the more precious. The consequent population explosion, however, demanded a planned solution to balance the scarcity of space, water, and sustenance. So a computerized system of lots had been developed by the IVT known as occupant disposal, politely alluded to by its acronym OD, whereby individuals selected at random, generally but not always of retirement age, were notified of their disposal order. Compliance was compulsory at the specified time and date. There were no appeals or reprieves.

*

Mrs. Marble realized she must have fallen asleep, when she heard the sound of the front sliding door lock click open.—"Is that you, Elgin?"

Two plain clothes men crowded her bedroom doorway. "Agent Belfry," the tall one flashed a badge. "Agent Quirt." nodded his squat partner.

"Where's Elgin?" she asked.

"That's what we'd like to know, Ma'am!" Belfry replied.

"Coop up now!" Quirt winked.

"Appreciate your cooperation!" Belfry translated.

Flustered and a bit embarrassed, Ellen switched off the whispering hologram of her husband and straightened her clothes as the agents watched impatiently. They followed her to the living nook.

"Please have a seat," she said.

They remained standing.

"It's 15:33, where's your son?" Belfry snapped.

"Elgin ought to be home from school any minute

now." she assured them with a bit too much conviction.

"Come off it Missy, he ain't been to school!" Quirt curtly informed her.

"There must be some mistake." she said.

"You don't mind if we have ourselves a look around, do you?" Belfry asked, not waiting for a reply.

"What's this all about!?" Ellen demanded, as the agents rummaged through the apartment.

"In here!" Quirt called from Elgin's room.

"Right!" Belfry, who'd been inspecting her hologram boxes, turned on his heels.

Ellen followed.

She found Quirt fingering Elgin's tin can train.— "Interesting gizmo, wouldn't you say?"

"A multi-car elevator prototype, rather primitive!" she grinned, "His father was an EO."

"Ever see a horizontal elevator?" Quirt grinned.

"Horizontal, definitely horizontal—quite like a train!" Belfry concurred.

7.

"Elgin!" cried an excited confederate, Skip Skyscraper, nicknamed Scraper, "Look at what I found!"

Elgin shone a high-power torch taken from his father's stash of elevator tools.

Scraper held up a round object covered by a cracked clear plastic cap, with the letters N, W, S, and E marked on its surface and a trembling needle that kept stubbornly pointing in one direction however much you tilted or turned it.

They'd been rummaging around in the vicinity of one of those disaffected elevator shafts in an off-limits zone designated as an archeological. Like countless other such sites, the proliferation of which exceeded the limited capabilities of the understaffed Institute for Archeological Investigation, an IVT affiliate, this one too lay fallow. The law prohibited demolition and drilling at any site until such time as the block archeologists had a chance to sift the rubble for forbidden relics of horizontal intent, all of which were to be retrieved for study in temporary museums reserved for IVT-accredited scholars (to which, in any case, the general public was barred access) and subsequent disposal. The considerable time lapse between the official designation of an archeological site and its sequestering and inspection by the IVT created an opportunity for amateur collectors to step in and scavenge for spoils.

*

"What you got there, son?" A beam of light

struck Scraper full in the face.

The boys looked up in horror, ready to run if they spotted the ivy hue of an IVT uniform. They were somewhat relieved, though still on their guard, when an old man with a sack on his back came limping toward them. Had he followed them, or had he been there all along, watching from the dark?

"It's mine!" Scraper closed his hand tightly around the object and with the raised fist made a threatening gesture.

"Don't worry, fellah, Cornelius is no common thief! My ancestors ran clipper ships and trains. Current circumstances compel me to eke out my humble existence as an antique dealer. If you'll be so good as to show me that little trinket I may be able to identify it and tell you what it's worth!"

"Go ahead, Scraper!" Elgin urged. "What good does it do us if we don't even know what it is?"

"Bright boy!" the stranger nodded.

Reluctantly, Scraper opened his clenched fist, ready to strike out with his left should the old man try to grab it.

"Let's have a look," the man hobbled closer and drew a curious pair of glasses out of his coat pocket, one lens of which was red and the other blue. He did not put the glasses on, but merely dangled them by their frames.

PETER WORTSMAN

"Can I try those on, Mister?" Scraper asked.

"Perhaps," the old man smiled. "But what assurance can you give me that I will get them back?"

–"I could let you hold this thingamajig."

–"Now there's a fair proposition!"

Scraper snatched the glasses and tossed Cornelius the round object.

"Careful, boy!" the old man shouted, catching his precious prize an inch above the rubble-strewn ground. "My my!" he muttered to himself, laying his treasure flat in the palm of his hand, momentarily oblivious to the boys' presence.

Scraper put on the glasses. "They sure make things look funny!" he laughed. "It's like I've popped a pleasure pill!" And he went skipping off among the rubble, delighted with the trade.

Elgin, meanwhile, watched the old man with equal parts interest and distrust. Noticing Elgin's gaze out of the corner of his eye, Cornelius looked up with a smile. Each had sized up the other and decided that there was more there than meets the eye. The old man realized that he had foolishly let on too much about himself and the value of the object in question whereas the other boy, entranced as he was by those worthless 3D spectacles, would have been an easy touch, he still had to contend with his savvy partner.

"What is it?" Elgin inquired.

–"It's a compass."

–"What's it for?"

–"It tells you which way you're going."

"What other way is there than up and down?" Elgin asked with a wary thrill.

The old man knew there was no point lying. "The letters," he said, "refer to the four directions, north, east, south and west," pointing as he spoke. "Way back when," he added with a solemn expression, "travelers used a compass to get their bearings. This one," he observed, "was probably a toy."

–"How do you know?"

–"The figure in the middle, it's a mouse."

–"So!?"

–"The plastic cover's brittle, the casement flimsy. Besides which, it's inappropriate, considering the nature of the site. Evidently," he said, pointing to the high domed ceiling and the remains of a large clock on the wall, its hour hand melted and minute hand twisted, as though from a terrible explosion, "this was not a forest or a tundra!"

"Evidently!" Elgin mimicked Cornelius' sarcastic tone.

"Look around you!" the old man said with a quaking voice of excitement, shining his beam upwards toward a high vaulted ceiling. "Do you know what this place was?"

Elgin looked long and hard. Only then did he realize that he had never before set foot in a space so vast, with quite as much headroom above and elbow room around him. The old man swung his power torch in circles round his head. All around them there were portals with paint peeling off arched passageways. One to which the faded latex still clung bore the inscription: T ACK 21. Elgin trembled, excited to be surrounded by so much empty space, terrified lest the ceiling suddenly collapse. Instinctively he fell to his knees, stooped forward and folded his arms over his head, as he'd been taught to do in school in the event of a block attack.

"This way!" the old man motioned. And as in a dream, Elgin followed him toward the portal with the mysterious inscription. Cornelius stooped down on the way and scooped up a snippet of thin cardboard and handed it to Elgin, who thrilled at the touch. Paper products were a rarity in a world of plastic. Able to make out the letters B…U…F… F…A…L…O, printed in faded blue, Elgin was puzzled. The buffalo, he remembered from vertical history, was a big fuzzy foraging animal now long since extinct, generally associated with a wide open space called the Great Plains. Perhaps this place had been a park or zoo.

"What is it?" Elgin asked, breathless.

The old man laughed. "It's a ticket, boy."

–"A ticket to what?"

"To *where?*" the old man corrected.

"I don't understand," Elgin confessed.

"Look out there, boy! What do you see?" The old man shone his torch into the channel of darkness on the far side of the portal.

"A tunnel!" Elgin gasped. It was lined on the ground by two rusty parallel metal rails with wooden beams laid out between them and bolted together at regular intervals.

"Tracks!" the old man whispered.

"This place then…?" Elgin asked with awe.

"A station, a train station, the greatest of them all…all…all," the old man's voice echoed in the tunnel. "Grand Central Station!" he cried out, scampering along the track. "And that way," he pointed, after studying the object in his hand, "is north!"

"North…north…north…!" the sound echoed in the darkness long after the old man had disappeared.

II

1.

When Elgin got home he found his mother weeping.

–"Mom, what is it?!"

Ever since his father's disposal, he had taken a gentler tone with her, as if she, not he, needed protecting.

Her joy at seeing her son safe was overshadowed by a dark dread of what lay in store for him. "They came here looking for you. I told them you were at school!"

Elgin grinned. "It's nice to know somebody missed me."

"Oh Elgin," she broke out crying, "you don't understand the seriousness of the matter!"

"What's the good of being young," he said, "if you take things too seriously?"

"I went to see Dr. Orion," she replied.

–"How is he?"

–"He showed me your block citizenship composition."

–"Didn't he find it vertical enough?"

–"For up's sake, Elgin, don't you know you're skating on thin ice!"

–"So what if I slip? I'll freefall all the way to China!"

–"They're talking about a personality profile, Elgin. Do you know what that means?"

–"Fame and fortune?" His flip tone camouflaged his own mounting upset.

–"After a PP, the next step is compulsory desensitization!"

–"All the kids go through desensitivity training, Mom, it's no big deal!" Elgin shrugged. "It's a character-shaping experience!" he mouthed the popular slogan with a grin.

*

After evening nourishment, Mrs. Marble found her son packing his father's old leisure backpack with a nervous determination.

–"What are you doing? Where are you going?"

"Camping," he said, without blinking.

She hugged him to her. "They took your train, you know!"

"They haven't got enough imagination to make it run!" he smiled.

There was silence between them, not the empty electric silence sputtering between Inter-Eye segments, but a heavy human silence choked with emotion.

"I love you, Mom!" the boy said, gripping the backpack.

She shut her eyes to hold back the tears and preserve an intact image of her son, for he wouldn't be leaving a hologram of himself behind.

2.

Agents Belfry and Quirt were waiting in the corridor several doors down. They always gave their mark a little lead for, like all predators, they enjoyed the chase. But that was not the only reason they allowed Elgin to make a run for it. Small fry, like Elgin, however tasty, had hardly enough meat on their bones to be worth the effort, whereas if they gave him some slack he might very well lead them to a bed of Crabs.

3.

Dr. Orion made it a regular practice to round out each sustained up-cycle (or what his pupils called the old *tick-tock*) with a well-earned downtime visit to his favorite horizon parlor. He was feeling eminently vertical following his meeting with Mrs. Marble, the dead level bitch. A mother who fails to keep her child in check deserves no pity. Quite the contrary, it was his official duty to correct her mistakes. Inappropriate parental imprints do lasting damage on their precious pups. How lovely it was to watch her wriggle. It was his duty, after all, as high school principal, to sift out the bad seed so as to protect the rest so prone to spoilage. He himself would be conducting the PP on the boy, a responsibility he took very seriously. But there was time enough to muse on such official business.

Although tolerated, horizon parlors were not altogether respectable, and patrons of social standing like himself concerned for their reputations generally hid behind an alternate identity conferred by an accommodating hostess, just in case the list of clients should be leaked to the ever-eager Inter-Eye for their weekly Subverted Verticality Report, a favorite down-time feature. So Mr. Orion checked in as Orville Wright, a sobriquet further shortened to Or by a plucky hostess.

"Where to today, Or?" she asked.

"I don't know," he hesitated, scanning the electronic menu of virtual destinations. Hawaii, Singapore, Sri Lanka, Fiji, Staten Island—the names evoked no vivid associations, the globe having long since been subdivided into homogeneous numbered blocks with no distinguishing mark.

"Urban, suburban or rural?" she pressed, the magma of impatience evident in her voice beneath her studied professional smile.

PETER WORTSMAN

"I just can't make up my mind," he admitted, reverting to a childish indecisiveness the hostess found galling.

"How about a historical junket?" she recommended, putting her smile and perkiness on automatic pilot. "Our ever-popular whirlwind tour of the sin cities includes unforgettable glimpses of Sodom, Rome, Bangkok, Las Vegas and Atlantic City."

"Perhaps," he said.

–"Or maybe you prefer the Penal Colonies Tour? Participant or spectator, handcuffs or leg irons, the choice is yours."

Dr. Orion perked up.

*

He always traveled in style. He liked such little extras as a hot towel and a glass of bubbly to still the jitters prior to departure.

"I'm your hostess, you may call me Miss!" a stern-looking schoolmarm with hair pulled back in a tight knot introduced herself. "You will be physically restrained for the duration of the trip."

"There must be some mistake," he protested meekly.

"This way!" she pointed, her index finger trembling with impatience.

Resistance was futile. Dr. Orion permitted himself to be pinioned to a reclining chair in a private Pullman car, all the amenities of which were just out of reach.

"Champagne, please, Miss!" he requested.

The hostess popped open a bottle and poured herself a glassful and drank it down. "Not bad!" she said.

–"May I have a sip?"

Frowning, she found a funnel in the minibar. "Open your mouth!" she said and proceeded to pour the rest of the bottle down his throat, so that what he did not gag on soaked his clothes.

"Hot towel!" he pleaded.

With a pair of pincers she plucked a steaming hot hand towel from a metal box and dropped it on his face, nearly scalding his delicate pink skin.

"All aboard," she cried, "for the Penal Colony Express!" The simulated train whistle blew. The wood-paneled wall opened to reveal an interactive screen with simulated old-fashioned outdoor landscape, including occasional cattle and waving children, rushing by like canned memories, in the opposite direction.

First stop Andersonville, where the starving prisoners on screen begged for food and Dr. Orion, opting for the role of prison guard, was released from his straps and took considerable pleasure in stuffing sawdust down their mouths.

At Devil's Island, Dr. Orion switched places and had himself stripped and shackled to a treadmill and made to drag considerable loads at a rapid clip. Whenever he slowed down, Miss made a simulated whip crack in stereo, stinging realistically, though it raised no welts.

Next stop, Auschwitz!

Dr. Orion watched the screen as an old coal burning engine coughed out a filthy black cloud, spitting steam, and a towering gateway came into view. The moving image slowed down to a crawl and came to a dead stop at a railroad siding accompanied by the snarl and bark of savage dogs.

"I think I'll sit this one out," he whispered.

"As you like," a sexless voice said.

Other simulated passengers were herded out of the train to the welcome of dogs and bludgeon-wielding black-booted guards. The passengers were separated into two lines, one to the right and one to the left. The reluctant were prodded and shoved. Infants were torn out of their mother's arms and swung, head first, against the rusted metal railing of the cattle car they came in, then flung into a lifeless heap. The sight was a little too messy for Dr. Orion's taste.

"Fast forward, please," he muttered.

"Too horizontal for your taste?!" Miss teased.

Now he watched eagerly as the women and girls undressed, and shivered as they were herded into a small square chamber, imagining himself pressed between bosom and buttocks.

A few seconds of the spectacle of asphyxiation was all he cared for.

"Please!" he whimpered.

But at Srebenize he made up for lost time, an enthusiastic participant in the simulated rape of young girls, complete with realistic screams, as the families of victims looked on.

All in all, he had had a splendid time.

Dr. Orion came away feeling refreshed and ready to tackle the challenges of the coming *tick tock*.

4.

As Elgin headed for the elevators, he thought he heard footsteps behind him. Turning, he saw no one following him. He reflected a moment on whether to take the passenger elevator, in which the Inter-Eye monitor would immediately register his presence, or to ride the freight, whose operator, an old friend of his father's, would not ask too many questions. His dad had taken him along on many a freight run to teach him the ropes, so the elevator repair crews were well accustomed to his presence and might accept this little lapse from protocol as a residual surplus of filial devotion or advance training for a future career.

"How's it riding, son?" Otis, his father's longtime partner and subsequent replacement on the freight run, greeted him with a warm welcoming smile.

"Smooth as silk," Elgin gave the customary response and Otis waved him in.

—"Where to, chief?"

—"Oh, I don't know, I thought maybe I'd take a simulated hike on Sub-Sub-17."

—"Capital idea, son! Used to go hiking myself… me 'n your old…" Otis swallowed the end of his sentence. It wasn't good form to make direct reference to the recently disposed. Only survivors had a limited license to do so for a two-week period of mourning.

"Dad was an avid artificialist," Elgin nodded. "He knew every simulated bird call in the book!"

Seeing as the boy had breached the subject and there was no one else around, Otis felt free to reminisce, an incorrigible but understandable habit for a man who spent most of his time in a box going up and down. "Your dad taught me every darn thing I know about elevators. People think it's all technology, just nuts 'n bolts. Nothing could be farther from the truth. Elevator man's gotta respect his box. It's his second home! He's got to listen to the cables, they'll tell him everything he needs to know. It's like your dad always used to say: 'When you hear the cables singin' you better be sure they're singin' in tune!' He had what we like to call perfect cable pitch. Me, I'm not so well endowed. Got to work at it."

As the elevator went slinking downwards, Elgin did not mind the man's jabbering—so long as he asked no questions.

–"Dad said you'n he practically went back to the Walk-Up days together!"

–"Not that far, son. But I will tell you this: There ain't a box in the block me 'n Upton ain't rode 'n repaired, 'n that's a fact! He always said you had the makings of a…"

"Say, Otis," Elgin cut him short in a conspiratorial whisper, "you ever been down to the digs?"

Otis blinked. Small infractions from the rules like letting Elgin ride the freight for old time's sake didn't rock the box, but he made it a practice to steer clear of certain taboo topics. Nobody talked about the digs. Nobody who wanted to stay on the right side of the law, away from the 13th Floor.—"Not that it's any of my business, boy, but ain't you supposed to be learning your lessons?"

"Special dispensation," Elgin was quick to improvise. "Archeology Club's going on an expedition next week and I'm sort of scouting out the territory."

"Got ya!" Otis nodded, not believing a word of it, but inclined to keep his nose out of other people's business. It was better, he thought, to go on making small talk until the kid was out of his box. "Upton always said you had the makings of a topnotch elevator man and I'm inclined to agree."

–"Thanks, Otis."

–"With your brains, I bet you could make it to supervisor, maybe block inspector!"

They had dropped down below Sub-Sub-7 and were soon entering the security levels separating the zone of habitation from the artificial wildlife sanctuary on Sub-Sub-17.

"Otis," Elgin tried to make his request sound as matter-of-fact as possible, "would you mind very much letting me out at Sub-Sub-11? That's where we're going to be going on the school dig next week."

The elevator man solemnly shook his head.— "Sorry, I can't do that, son, 'less you can show me your authorization disc."

Elgin reached into his backpack.—"Damn!" he said, after a calculated period of rummaging, I must have left it at school."

"No AD, no exit!" The elevator man reverted to an official tone.

–"Please, Otis, for old time's sake!"

—"Listen, son, your father 'n me, we were friends, but he's gone down the shoot, 'n I ain't plannin' on joinin' him any time soon if I can help it. Don't wanna go back to 13 neither!"

"Back!?" Elgin looked stunned.

"Youthful infraction," the elevator man nodded, terror written all over his face.

—"What did you do, Otis, hijack a freight?!"

—"Fellah slipped me a pleasure voucher. 'Finest horizon parlor in the block!' he swore. I was 18 and I'd never set foot in one. All I had to do was to make a special delivery of a package. I made the delivery alright, only I was the package! IVT undercover set me up. Got myself an all expense paid week's getaway to the 13th Floor. They let me out on account of my clean record and my youth. But I'll tell you this much: my dreams have been perfectly vertical ever since. The cat done killed all my curiosity."

Elgin realized he had no other recourse now but the truth.—"I'll be perfectly vertical with you, Otis. I'm not going on an archeo-dig."

"Didn't think you was," Otis smiled to save face.

—"I'm in trouble, Otis. IVT searched the apartment. They're looking for me."

—"Tough break, son."

--Help me, please, Otis, for my father's sake!"

Otis thought fast. "I'm a damn fool," he said,

shaking his head, shifting to manual, and simulating a malfunction that made the elevator jump. "I know you know how to run this box, boy! You let me out at the last inhabited floor. I'll tell 'em you had a wrench. Better bop me on the back of the head, 'n make it look convincing!"

Elgin gave the elevator man a hug, feeling at that moment as if through him he were hugging his father's memory.

Otis wasn't feeling sentimental, only wary, when he stopped the elevator.—"Go ahead, boy, bop me, hard! From here on in you're on your own."

Elgin struck the elevator man from behind, hard enough to leave a big red bump as Otis tumbled out onto the floor at Sub-Sub-3. Sub-Sub-3 was the seedy zone where residents down on their luck, responsibility shirkers, and those suspected of latent diagonal tendencies lived. Many were hardened veterans of repeated visits to the 13th Floor. Luckily, no one was around to notice.

Elgin smiled sadly to himself as he kicked the elevator man's boots clear of the closing doors and lowered the lever gently. "Look at me, daddy," he half-cried, half-laughed, "I'm an elevator man!" The tears came rolling down like a cloudburst of simulated rain on a smiling neon noon. Elgin let go and started sobbing as the elevator dropped. It felt good to be crying in free fall.

5.

Deeply concerned for her son's sake, Ellen Marble decided on a desperate measure. Still a slender, handsome woman at 45, she could make heads turn if she put her mind and makeup to it.

*

"Mrs. Marble!?" Dr. Orion was momentarily stunned to find her at the door of his residential cube, with her coat open, at this late hour. "To what do I owe this…unexpected pleasure?"

A seasoned horizon hostess when she and Upton Marble met 17 years ago, though she had since been promoted to a supervisory capacity, monitoring the propensities of high profile parlor patrons, she still knew what men seek on simulated long-distance trips. Having kept her figure intact, she fit into her stretchy old red uniform, low cut with a slit all the way up to her right hip, and one long plastic zipper that wound its way around like a Christmas candy cane. The iridescent shimmer of the gown had faded some, and the material had wrinkled a bit along the path of the zipper but the effect could still be quite tantalizing.

"I hope I'm not disturbing you," she flashed him a disarming smile.

Worried lest any of the neighbors notice his guest, Dr. Orion pulled her in.

"Do sit down." he said, focusing on the dimples in her knees, anxiously dabbing his brow with the sleeve of his dressing gown, while with the back of his hand shoving back the spectacles that kept sliding over the oily bridge of his nose. She was practiced at crossing her legs.

A man of his position, whose decisions affected young destinies, and by extension, their entire extended family units, could expect an occasional visit from a distraught parent offering a wide variety of products and services. And Dr. Orion was not averse to accepting a little favor every now and again, to which his superiors turned a blind eye. Discretion was the only rule.

–"Now then, Mrs. Marble, how can I... help you?"

–"Loneliness, Dr. Orion, is a terrible thing."

–"Indeed!"

–"Well, you see, Mr. Marble and I, we were very happy together!"

–"I'm sure you were...responsibly fond of the disposed."

–"It's so...hard now without him."

–"He did his duty. Better to view disposal as a privilege than a duty! You must be quite devoted to your son."

–"Naturally, but devotion and…needing…are two different creatures."

–"I wouldn't know, Mrs. Marble, I've never been personally attached. My work takes up all my time."

She decided to be brash. "You do patronize the parlors, Dr. Orion, don't you?"

He blanched.

–"I can always tell a parlor man!"

"Oh?" the principal replied uncomfortably.

"You're very vertical!" she winked.

"Am I?" he replied, his vanity touched.

"Oh, yes!" she said, uncrossing and re-crossing her legs. "We all need a horizontal release every now and then to keep us on the straight and narrow!"

He tried not to notice her knees, over which the slit of her gown had slid ever higher, and looked her straight in the eye, reasserting his dominance. "Your son is in trouble, Mrs. Marble. If you think for a moment that you're coming here to see me might sway my judgment in any way, you're quite mistaken."

"Elgin's no angel, I know," she shrugged, "but surely a little childish indiscretion can be overlooked."

"On the contrary, Mrs. Marble, childish indiscretion, as you call it, is the first sign of trouble. I have put in an official request for a personality profile, which as you must know, will very likely lead to compulsory desensitization, an option which, quite frankly, you ought to have considered for the boy's sake long ago."

"But isn't there some way a mother can…make amends for her boy's failings?" she inquired, playing with the hook of her zipper.

–"I'm afraid you've got the wrong idea, Mrs. Marble!"

"Have I?" she whispered, dragging the zipper down from her left shoulder an inch or two across her breast.

"That's quite enough!" he wiped his brow and shoved back his foggy glasses.

"I was only getting warmed up…" she grinned.

Dr. Orion could control himself no longer. He reached out and tore at the zipper and the tiny imbedded beads of reconstituted musk exploded in its path. The dress pealed off easily like the skin of a banana, leaving a diagonal pink zipper track on her bare skin. He grabbed hold of her hair and, pressing her head down between his legs, slapped her bare bottom—"Suck!" he said, for he could not bear intimacy.

*

"You understand of course," he clarified, wiping the wetness off the vinyl sofa, once this unseemly display was over and done with, showing his zipped up guest to the door, "I can make no promises. The situation is delicate. Discretion is advised. But should you wish to discuss the matter again with me in private at some future date, I assure you that I would be only too happy to—how shall I put it?—appreciate your position."

–"By which you mean to say exactly what, Dr. Orion?"

–"By which I mean to say: Good downtime, Mrs. Marble!"

6.

"Sub-Sub-5, Sub-Sub-6, Sub-Sub-7…" Elgin counted out loud, and for a moment contemplated shifting to ultra-speed and dropping through the excavated layers of life all the way down to the great hole of China.

China in popular parlance was the ultimate bottom, more a concept than a place, since no one had ever been down so deep and returned to tell. Children reversed the word, calling it Anich, imagining a place where men stand on their heads and everything is topsy-turvy. Anich, young children were given to believe, was where the dearly disposed landed to start a new upside-down life. Anich balls, or nich-balls for short, a favorite toy made of compressed artificial rubber interspersed with microscopic air pockets so as to return the shock of impact with virtually undiminished force, never stopped bouncing.

Children were naturally petrified and thrilled at the prospect of abutting parallel blocks in the netherworld far down below. Cautionary nursery tales were told of a labyrinth of mirrors, and of a foolhardy boy who descended to China in search of a lost Anich ball and remains lost forever in the elusive maze of glass and illusion.

At Sub-Sub-9, Elgin suddenly got scared and shifted to manual, pulling the lever gently toward him as the cables sang and the falling box slowed down little by little, halting suddenly at Sub-Sub-11. Easy does it! his father would have said.

Elgin listened and smelled. Just yesterday, when he and Scraper had stumbled on the dig, the mustiness had been rich and unadulterated, the virgin darkness sliced by beams of their high power torches, the ultimate antithesis of a blanket of freshly fallen simulated snow in the Himalaya Towers. But now Elgin noticed the lingering odor of dynamite and the flicker of glow-dots, electronic fire flies which destruction crews – the "archies" – flung out by the handful to scatter light on a clean-up operation. No doubt about it, the archeologists had been back, and might still be about. Elgin would have to keep his power torch off and play blind, feeling his way slow-ly through the rubble of the station toward T ACK 21. If only the ceiling holds, he prayed.

How sloppy the archies were in their demolition. You would have thought that they at least harbored a certain inverted interest in the places and things they were trained to destroy. A taste for forbidden fruit. But for the most part, like children, the men on the dig simply delighted in the act of destruc-tion. Only on express orders from above did they ever bother to gather specimens for the Institute's revolving collection of past excesses, none of which were open for public viewing. These artifacts were analyzed by trained horizontalists, licensed experts with security clearance, whose detailed reports were subsequently filed away in IVT memory banks, and the objects themselves promptly pulverized. Occa-sionally, the scavengers got there first and sifted the rubble, considering the black market rate of return for horizontal memorabilia to be well worth the risk.

From time to time, the IVT saw fit to leak an archeological report on Inter-Eye, to feed the public taste for scandal and reinforce the fear of capture. Parents sent their offspring to bed early (though some daring tykes managed to sneak a peak) while Mom and Dad watched with a righteous indigna-tion (spiced with a voyeuristic tingle) at the deca-dent spectacle of exploding suspension bridges and, most especially, tunnels.

"Our forefathers were a frivolous lot," the Inter-Eye commentators solemnly insisted on the accompanying voice-over. "Heady with a sense of surplus space and careless of diminishing resources, they consumed themselves in a final feeding frenzy. In the rubble of their excesses we built up a perfect world. Having progressed beyond the primitive horizontal drive of homo-erectus, we have no need to scuttle along repulsively from place to place. Man was not made to crawl like a crab in the mud, but to stand upright and reach for the stars! Stay tuned and stand tall!"

These reports invariably concluded with the chase, entrapment and taped confession of a suspected *CRAB*.

*

–"Stop *CRAB*!"

The station was suddenly flooded with crisscrossing spotlights. Blinded, Elgin stumbled on an overturned wooden bench and fell. Unharmed, he lay face down with his hands folded over his head, as he'd seen the hunted do so many times on Inter-Eye. Seconds passed, and to his surprise and guarded relief he had not yet been apprehended. What's keeping them? he wondered. Hearing the echo of voices, he rolled over and dared open his eyes a crack. The great domed ceiling looked like the inside of a giant cracked eggshell with spotlights sweeping its surface, scooping out the soft egg white beneath the darkness.

The rousing theme music of Inter-Eye reports reverberated against the dome.

"Good downtime!" said an announcer, his voice echoing, too, until the soundmen made the necessary technical modifications. "This is John Hancock Tower, Jr. reporting to you live from the dark dank bowels of Block 367790, where archeologists are engaged in the systematic study and destruction of an ancient train station, and not just any station, ladies and gentlemen, but the one they once called Grand Central. The demolition has proved fruitful in other respects too. For the destruction team stumbled on a hornet's nest, or more aptly, a bed of *CRABS*, helping IVT agents nab a nasty King *CRAB*. Stay tuned for his live confession—after this…!"

Sucking in the air, after having held his breath for far too long and nearly fainted, Elgin could hardly believe his ears. They hadn't been after him at all, didn't even know he was there. With great effort he suppressed an urge to laugh out loud. Elgin just lay there staring at the ceiling, with a front row seat on breaking news in the making.

Again the Inter-Eye theme echoed against the dome.

The voice that followed sounded familiar, if a bit muffled, maybe drugged: "My name is Corne-

lius Vanderbilt XIII, and I am a convicted Crab!"
Guilty theme music played. "For years I have been
shamelessly undermining the vertical foundation
of society for personal profit. I ask neither for your
understanding nor for your mercy. I know that I
will get what's coming to me. I welcome…" The
sobriety of the staged confession was broken by a
sudden burst of laughter, and Elgin could not resist
the temptation to peak over the edge of the bench
and watch as the apprehended man broke loose, a
microphone dangling round his neck, and bounded into the mouth of the tunnel, still laughing as a
spotlight located him.—"I welcome the relief from
your vertical hell!" he cried.

"Cut!" shouted the director of the operation, as
the security detail turned their laser eliminator on
the fugitive, who promptly ceased to be.

"Up in a puff of smoke," the announcer concluded cheerfully, "so much for old King *CRAB*!"

Elgin lowered his head back behind the fallen
bench, lay face down, and trembled.

III

1.

Arriving at his work cube bright and early uptime, Mr. Orion was pleased, as always, at the sight of his squeaky clean stainless steel desktop, perfectly bare, shimmering in the glow of efficiency, for seldom did he leave a dossier dangling from one uptime to the next. A man of firm resolve, he ran the palm of his hand across its cool smooth surface. The sensation of buffed and polished metal never failed to thrill him. It made him shed all human frailty and feel as strong as a steel girder, humanity's most perfect product. He eased himself into his hydraulic chair, whose form-fitting ergonomic design perfectly fitted the curve of his spine, sighing as he sank into position for a cycle of service. Devoid of clutter, his compact cube fit him like a mold. If only the vertical world and its weak links were as sleek and compliant as stainless steel, how wonderful life would be, he thought, and liked the thought so much he recorded it and decided to flash it all day for the edification of his malleable little charges on the Inter-Eye screens in every classroom. Dr. Orion collected his reflections and planned to issue them on educational disc someday.

It was only after he had concluded with a smile that everything was as it should be that he noticed the red blinking light on his own personal Inter-Eye screen. With some trepidation, he uttered his password: "Stainless!" and awaited the response.

"Dr. Orion," said the simulated secretary, "you are summoned to see Ms. Teak, immediately!"

A call to the Block Superintendent of Schools! Such a thing did not happen every day. Indeed, he had had the privilege only twice before in his professional life: the first time on the occasion of his appointment to the office of school principal, when the superintendent, then newly named, a former principal herself who'd risen through the ranks, personally congratulated him; and subsequently, to accept a citation of efficiency, on which occasion the superintendent had delegated the duty to a smug assistant, and Dr. Orion had felt snubbed. She could only have summoned him now to discuss the school performance model he had devised and submitted to her more than a month ago. Optimal productivity, he argued, could only be achieved by bold measures: reward the top ten percent and dispose of the bottom ten! Let the median battle it out! Thus mediocrity will become an anachronism and superiority pull the laggards to ever higher performance. The same model, of course, after being tested in the schools, could later be applied to the workplace.

Dr. Orion viewed himself as a visionary pedagogue. Proud of his plan, he felt quite certain that his bold ideas would take him all the way to the top, and who knows, perhaps one day to take the superintendent's place. The slowness of her response to such an unquestionably effective plan could only mean one of two things: either she was jealous and seeking to protect her fiefdom from competing originality, or else she was no longer performing up to par and it was time for her to be replaced.

"Cancel all my appointments!" he called out in passing to his simulated secretary on screen, and "make sure that my desk is polished, I noticed a scratch."

Bursting with expectation, Dr. Orion stepped into the high-speed express elevator reserved for the administration that shot him up to the 333rd floor in a matter of seconds, gulping to ease the pressure in his ears and patting his chest to still the swelling exciting. For he felt quite certain that destiny called.

"Principal Orion here to see Superintendent Teak!" he announced to the Inter-Eye screen on the 333rd floor, whereupon the steel gray doors of the Block Board of Education slid open. Striding boldly down the corridor leading to the superintendent's office, he felt as if all eyes must surely be upon him, envious, admiring, adulatory, fawning. No doubt his proposals had been circulated among the bureaucratic ranks and the timid yes-men and -women trembled to be in the presence of a man of steel resolve whose vision would soon streamline public education, and perhaps, society itself.

Superintendent Teak had an actual secretary, a wasteful frivolity in these highspeed times, he thought.

"Can I help you?" the bespectacled anachronism inquired, somewhat disdainfully, flicking her fingernails impatiently on the top of her desk.

"Principal Orion here to see Superintendent Teak, I have been summoned!" he snapped back in a stentorian voice befitting his status and meant to put her in her place.

"Have a seat." she responded coolly, pointing to a gray vinyl sofa.

Speechless, Dr. Orion did as he was told, though he made a show of studying his watch.

"The Superintendent will see you now," the secretary announced as soon as he was seated.

"Dead-level bitch!" thought Dr. Orion, rising slowly, I'll put her in her place soon enough!

The Superintendent did not rise or reach out her hand as he approached, but studied him with her steel blue gaze. Then Dr. Orion remembered hearing that she had been in an elevator crash some years back, and though she'd suffered no loss to her mental faculties, a spinal accident had rendered her immobile.

"Have a seat!" she said in a tinny voice.

Dr. Orion smiled as he sank into the chair in front of her desk.—"It's an unexpected surprise to be summoned to see you again, Superintendent. The last time I had the honor was…"

"Yes, yes!" she cut him short.

He assumed she meant to get right down to business, and that the business related to his proposal. "High performance," he started in, "is merely a function of reward and punishment, promotion and disposal. False mercy is a wobbly yardstick, don't you agree?"

"I don't know what you're talking about," she responded impatiently.

"My proposal," he replied, a bit nonplussed, but trying not to show it, "you have read it, I presume!"

"I have not." replied Dr. Teak. The piercing look she gave him and the very severity of her expression sent a tremor from his heart to his bladder, which he only now remembered he'd forgotten to empty in his haste.

"I assumed…" he replied, his tone getting more and more timid by the second.

"That was a false assumption, Mr….!" Dr. Teak searched the dossier spread open on her desk.

"*Dr.* Orion," he filled in the blank, squirming in his chair, crossing and uncrossing his legs, shoving his spectacles back up his nose, for agitation always made them slip.

"As to the matter of your pupil, Master Marble!" she muttered.

Though greatly surprised to have been called on such a minor disciplinary matter, Dr. Orion felt relieved to deflect the official fury from himself. "Then you concur with my recommendation for a personality profile? Anti-social types had best be weeded out early before they infect their fellows, don't you think! The parents are wholly to blame. Though the late disposed father was an elevator man, the boy's mother, a former horizon parlor hostess, a woman of low morals," he sneered, "has a latent diagonal leaning, which, quite irresponsibly, I'm afraid, she passed on to…"

Once again Dr. Teak cut him short. "The boy was in your charge, was he not?"

"*Was*?!" Dr. Orion looked dismayed.

"The boy *is* missing, didn't you know!?" she curtly reported. "I do hope they find him soon for your sake as well as his. You understand, of course, that you will be suspended from all official duties and forfeit all privileges, pending the conclusion of the investigation. You will make yourself available to the IVT investigators in charge of the case."

"Missing? Suspended?" he muttered the words in disbelief, obscenities in the language of a pedagogue, already picturing the school swarming with

IVT men and Inter-Eye reporters, knowing full well that even if the boy were found and he himself were cleared of any direct responsibility, he'd never live down the blot on his record and could kiss the prospect of advancement goodbye. Realizing all this in a flash, he lost bladder control.

"That will be all!" said Dr. Teak.

Dr. Orion shuffled along, leaving a wet trail on the polished parquet, oblivious to the humiliation and to the secretary's barely muffled snicker, thinking only of how his professional future, or the little there was left to salvage of it, was linked to Elgin Marble.

2.

The IVT caught up with Scraper soon enough. Peddling trinkets from the Grand Central Station site, he foolishly tried to interest two plain clothed undercover agents in a pair of 3D glasses. "Guaranteed to make you see things in a new light!"

The taller of the two appeared to be interested.

"Or maybe you'd prefer the torn stub of a one-way ticket to Kalamazoo. It's very valuable," Scraper confided in a whisper, "but I got to dump it on account of it's hot."

"Glad to take the goods off your hands, son!" the

short man grinned, flashing an IVT badge, and introducing himself as Agent Quirt.

Scraper tried to run for it, but the taller of the two fired a detention dart, drawing a wave of inertia from the boy's own limitless reserves, freezing him in his tracks. "Another move and you're inert matter, son!" Agent Belfry added cheerfully.

Knowing he was trapped, Scraper sank to his knees.

Quirt grabbed the glasses. "Where'd you get the funny specs, kid?"

–"From a toy store, where else!"

"From a toy store, *Sir!*" Quirt corrected, kicking Scraper in the groin. Scraper howled.

"My colleague can make this experience very memorable for you, if you like," Agent Belfry advised.

"Let me repeat the question: Where'd you steal the specs?" Quirt continued the interrogation.

–"I didn't steal 'em, I swear, I just picked 'em up off the ground!"

"Stellar citizen, what!?" Belfry nodded. "Every litter bit hurts."

"That's right!" Scraper grinned.

"Hey kid, you dropped something," Quirt pointed to the ground at his feet, and when Scraper looked down, he gave him a swift kick to the jaw, eliciting a crack.

Scraper would have collapsed in pain if the detention dart had allowed him to. Instead, the pain throbbed, like a memory that refused to recede into the past.

"Where were we?" Belfry calmly inquired.

"We were having ourselves a nice conversation with this dear boy about bootlegged archeological specimens," Quirt shook his head, "when I got this inexplicable knee-jerk reaction to lying."

"Alright," Scraper conceded, in between moans, "I got it at a dig."

"Which dig?" asked Belfry.

"I don't remember, honest!" Scraper gave a pleading look.

"I'm sure you'd rather not have my friend refresh your memory!" Belfry warned.

"Grand Central!" Scraper shouted, "Grand Central Station!"

"Crab Country!" Belfry flashed a telling look.

Scraper shook his head in adamant denial. "We're scavengers is all!"

"*We?*" Quirt smiled in delight, clearly enjoying himself.

–"Me 'n Elgin! It was Elgin's idea! I just went

along for the kicks!"

"Smuggling is a serious matter, son!" Belfry gave the boy a solemn look.

Scraper was feeling desperate. "Smuggling was just a sideline!" he volunteered.

"A sideline?" Quirt's interest was peaked.

"Elgin said I could keep the booty." Scraper blubbered on. "He was looking for an escape route, a tunnel."

"Tunnel?" Quirt perked up.

"Did he locate one?" Belfry responded with sober excitement.

"I didn't stick around to find out!" the boy shook his head. The wave of inertia was lifting, the strength returning to his legs. Scraper felt a little bad about having snitched on Elgin, but he had no doubt Elgin would have done the same, under the circumstances, or maybe he already had.—"Can I go now, Sir?"

"I don't see why not." Belfry shrugged.

But Quirt hadn't finished with him yet. "Your glasses, son!" he said, holding them out, and when Scraper reached out, dropping them an inch short of his hand. Scraper bent down to retrieve them and the agent brought the heel of his boot down hard.— "See ya 'round, kid!"

PETER WORTSMAN

3.

Not daring to budge long after the Inter-Eye camera crew called it quits, curled up like an unborn fetus, Elgin lay beside the overturned bench in total darkness, replaying recent events. Faces flashed past his mind's eye: his father in chloroformed repose, not a care in the world, being wheeled out to the disposal chute; his mother, lips clamped, as custom prescribed, holding back the tears; the neighbors nodding, flashing false sympathetic smiles to hide their relief that someone else had been selected; the face of the derelict from Block 367789—"There are mind tunnels too!"—What did he mean?; Scraper grinning, always up for a lark, the snot forever running down his nose like lava from a live volcano—; Cornelius, the fancy scavenger; the compass, face with four eyes and a revolving needle for a nose; Otis, in terror—"Ain't about to risk a return to 13!"; T ACK 21; the old man scurrying down the track—"Relief!"—Here one minute, gone the next in a puff of smoke—"Relief from your vertical hell!..."

The earth and the rubble felt cool and strangely comforting. Like a toy crane, Elgin's curled fingers idly dug and dumped, dug and dumped. Accustomed from many a scavenging expedition, he felt no fear of the dark. On the contrary, he breathed easy under its blanket of invisibility, protecting him from the prods of the vertical world: from the dullness and drivel of school with the principal's foolish reflections flashing on the Inter-Eye screen in between bells; from the intrusive simplicity of Herbert, Jr., the neighbor's boy; from the ache of his father's loss; and from the oppressive intensity of his mother's love.

It started the day his schoolmates played a trick on him, switching the signs of the boys and girls rooms. Rushing in, his bladder bursting, he caught an older girl squatting in an open stall with her knees drawn up to her chin and her panties dangling at her ankles. She was startled but didn't move to cover herself. And when he turned to leave, she reached out and grabbed his hand and pressed it between her legs. And though they had recently reviewed the principles of procreation and the strictly enforced laws of birth crime in class—couples selected by lottery were licensed to procreate once in the course of their union and all others were restricted from so doing, under penalty of neonatal confiscation and sterilization, lapses dropped down the ODC—this was different from the schematic diagrams in the exercise manual. And swaying gently back and forth, she held his hand against her, opening her legs and closing them again, opening and closing, opening and closing, till a taunting refrain outside: "Elgin's in the girl's room! Elgin's in the girl's room!" made him suddenly tear his fingers free. "Please!" she begged him. And not knowing what to do with his slimy wet hand, he slapped her in the face, perplexed then, as now, by the odd mix of sensations stirred up in him. She cried and he bounded out the door, running the gauntlet of giggling schoolboys.

Picturing the girl now, still curled up with his knees up to his chin, eyes shut tight, Elgin started rocking, pressing a hand between his legs, opening and closing, opening and closing, as she had done, playing both him and her. Only this time the darkness offered welcome refuge and no one butted in on the game.

4.

Ellen Marble had come to distrust knocks. At first she tried to pretend there was no one home. She was hardly delighted, though it did mitigate her terror, when she recognized the voice belonging to the insistent knuckles as those of the high school principal. Disgusted though she was at the thought of dealing with him again on any level, his unexpected appearance rekindled a flicker of hope that all was not lost for Elgin.

"Do come in, Dr. Orion." she said, forcing her lips to twist into a studied horizon parlor smile.

"Quick, Mrs. Marble! We must find Elgin!" he said, nearly tumbling to the ground as she opened the door, which he'd been leaning hard against, afraid of being seen.

Puzzled, to say the least, at the principal's sudden appearance and dreading another parent-teacher conference, she realized with a rush of relief and renewed trepidation that he was not there to "appreciate her position." Ellen Marble was no fool. If the principal took a sudden interest in Elgin, she knew full well it was not to please her or protect her son, but for some reason of his own, a reason more than likely involving a perceived threat to his position. And though she would have liked nothing better than to witness his official fall from grace, for the moment at least it was clear that their common interests demanded a temporary alliance. However wary, she could ill afford not to play along, at least until she'd sounded him out. It was not a matter of trust, but of expediency. All this she fathomed in a flash. The principal's problem hung like an electroleash round his neck, and she knew it, a leash whose handle she held firmly and that bound him to her and her to him, like pet and master, though both knew that the roles could be reversed at any moment.

"Why should I trust you?" she asked.

"My dear Mrs. Marble," he pleaded, falling to his knees, like a man about to propose marriage or beg for mercy, "though I may have behaved in a less than gentlemanly manner when last we met, your, how shall I put it, position having gotten the better

PETER WORTSMAN

of me, my professional conscience reasserted itself. Please believe me when I assure you of my genuine concern for your son's safety. A school principal is, after all, a surrogate father to the pupils in his charge."

—"Your paternal interest is touching, Dr. Orion! Let me remind you, though, that Elgin already has a father, more present in memory to him and to myself than you will ever be in person!"

—"You're quite right to revile me, Mrs. Marble! I can hardly blame you for that. But surely there is some way that I can make amends!"

—"Don't you think for a moment that I buy your bellyaching! But you know as well as I do that, more than anything else, I want to find my son and help him if I can. And, for some reason that escapes me at the moment, you want to find him too. Fine! But how do I know what you mean to do with him once you find him?!"

—"Alright, Mrs. Marble. Let me be perfectly vertical and lay it on the line. If I don't find your son before the IVT does, I can kiss my pedagogical career goodbye."

—"You know what else you can kiss, for all I care, Doctor!"

—"I'll make a deal with you, dear lady. Help me find Elgin, and I'll make sure the personality profile goes well for him."

–"Help him escape, Doctor!"

–"What are you saying?"

"The tunnels!" she replied without hesitation.

–"But for up's sake, you know as well as I do that they're nothing but an adolescent pipe dream."

The woman looked him hard in the face. "I worked the horizon parlors for 15 years. I read the minds of high profile guests, the kind that can afford to relax their vertical restraint and risk indiscretions. I know that the tunnels are real."

"Alright, Mrs. Marble, though I'm conceding the possibility of their existence, let's say, for argument's sake, I could get Elgin into one of your so-called tunnels, what good would it do him? It's a dead end! There's nowhere to go!"

"All my life," she said, "I've believed in some sweet elsewhere—call it China, call it heaven, call it New Jersey!"

–"That's storybook stuff, Mrs. Marble, the lies they tell children to lull them to sleep!"

"Along with the stalwart virtues of verticality?" she flashed a smile that almost immediately straightened into a cold hard look of determination. "You get him into a tunnel and I'll help you find him!"

"Deal," he said.

–"What assurance do I have, Dr. Orion?"

–"You have my word of honor, Mrs. Marble."

Whereupon she laughed, walked over to a drawer built into the wall, opened it, rummaged about for quite a while in search of something, and finally pulled out a pillbox.

"Take this!" she said, unscrewing the lid and removing a clear capsule.

–"What is it?"

–"Just a little sensory enhancer we used to use at the parlor to maintain stamina on simulated long-distance trips."

"Public officials are not licensed to take any stimulants while on duty!" he objected.

–"Am I to understand then that this is an official visit, Dr. Orion?"

He looked at her now like a naughty boy caught in the act, took the pill and swallowed it with a wariness born of lifelong discipline and restraint and a long sublimated longing for sensory release.

"Good boy!" she winked, and counted aloud to thirty. "Suggestive emotant: I will it, you feel it!"

–"How's that?"

"It's like the pain of birth-giving, only without the pay-off." she laughed.

He eyed her now with great trepidation.

"Just take a deep breath when it gets bad," she

shrugged. "The pill has a 24-hour effect. Understood?"

He nodded, waiting for the pain that did not come.

"I'll only be a minute," she said, rushing to the bedroom to change into traveling clothes.

Afraid of making a move, lest he set off the imagined spasms, he peered after her, wondering if he'd been had.

IV

1.

Desensitivity training, commonly known as DENT, culminated in a competition generally scheduled between the subject's 15th and 16th year, on a date set by the Behavior Regulation Commission of the Block Board of Education. Victorious candidates sometimes went on to professional careers in the sport. The training was not compulsory, though social norms and peer pressure made compliance virtually universal, with only a few holdouts. It was a proud day for parents and offspring. Invitations were sent out via Inter-Eye to family, friends, neighbors and co-workers. The party that followed the competition was as lavish as celebrants could afford.

Gladys Loyola counted the days until Herbert Jr.'s match. As floor chair of the IVT Ladies Auxiliary, it was up to her to set a good example.

"Oh, Ellen," she'd chirp to her neighbor whenever she ran into her. "I just can't wait. Herbert, Jr. is so ready!"

In secret, of course, like every mother, she feared the change, the sudden irreparable rupture in her link to the dear little lump of life she'd dropped and nurtured for all those years. It was a fear she could not share with Herbert, Sr., himself a high-level elevator operations supervisor and avid DENT enthusiast.

"Keep your head up! Give it everything you've got!" he smiled and gave his son a fatherly shove that sent him flying across the living cube. From early on, Herbert, Sr. was tough with his offspring, forever jabbing him in the ribs, coming up suddenly from behind with a headlock, tripping him when he wasn't looking.—"Never let down your guard! Preparedness is everything! You better believe it!"

To which, rubbing his bruises, Herbert, Jr. dutifully replied: "You bet, Dad!"

Gladys hid her apprehension behind the business of party preparations. "There's so much to do," she complained to Ellen, "so many details to keep in mind. Herbert, Sr. will be inviting all the vertical brass in the block. I've ordered a cake in the form of an express elevator with the words "Give 'Em Hell, Herbert, Jr.!" inscribed in blue. Everybody but everybody will be watching the match on Inter-Eye."

"I'm sure everything's going to be just fine," Ellen reassured her. It was considered bad form to speak of risks.

Beside herself the day of the scheduled match, Gladys knocked at her neighbor's door, but there was no answer. She tried repeatedly to reach her on Inter-Eye, but to no avail. Where could she possibly be?! Gladys fretted. She and Ellen had lived on the same floor since their simultaneous licensed inception, grown pigtails and turned cartwheels down the corridor, attracting the attention of the boys who craned their necks for a peak under their skirts. They'd gone through elementary indoctrination, IVT surveillance and horizon parlor hostess training together, and though Ellen had always been different from the others—"She's over-internal!" said Tilly Rushmore— Gladys had never held such evident character defects against her friend until now. How diagonal of her not to be there on the very day I need her most! Gladys thought, unable to conceive that her friend could possibly have any more pressing concerns.

*

The match was conducted in a regulation ceremonial elevator shaft. DENT teams from different floors competed for occupation and dominance of an old-fashioned hand-regulated Otis freight elevator fitted with removable panels above and below, suspended midway between the two competing floors. Whichever team commandeered the elevator and piloted it to their floor was declared the winner. Accidents did happen, careless candidates occasionally tripped and were crushed, or strangled by loose cables, or else sent hurtling to China. But the prospective humiliation and lifelong stigma of defeat far outweighed any risks for the contestants or their family units. For the losing team, the blight on their records severely limited any chances of social and professional advancement. And whereas the victorious team members had every hope of rising in the ranks, and remained forevermore loyal to their captain, whose influence he was honor-bound to apply on their behalf; the losers were often so dismayed at their loss that they turned on their captain and shoved him down the open shaft.

*

Gladys Loyala courageously held back her tears, straightening her son's DENT helmet and gear, as Herbert, Sr., gave him a last paternal shove out the door and into the hallway, where his teammates huddled in nervous anticipation. Because of Herbert, Sr.'s position, Herbert, Jr. had been named team captain.—"Show 'em what kind of stuff you're made of, son! Be vertical! Be proud!"

2.

–"Stay tuned, ladies and DENTs! Keep your Inter-Eye on the Junior DENT Championship Match of the season. Today the Spiders of the 159th Floor, so dubbed because of their outstanding webbing skills, take on the 157th Floor Climbers, famed for their rapid ascents. With me here in the booth is the greatest living DENTer of them all, Bobby Pyramid. Glad to have you with us, Bobby!"

–"Glad to be here, Biff!"

–"You played in some sensational DENT match-es, Bobby, and you sent many an unwitting opponent free-falling to China!"

–"Beautiful memories, Biff!"

–"Tell us, Bobby, what was your greatest match?"

–"Well, Biff, I'd have to say it was my first."

–"You mean as a kid?"

–"That's right, Biff. I've played professional DENT for more years than I care to recall, and then stepped back to report on it. But believe you me, your first DENT match is burnt into your memory banks!"

–"Tell us the highlights!"

–"Well, Biff, it was like this. When they knocked out our captain with an oil spill, I took command. 'Boys,' I said, 'there's only one way to beat those horizontal devils at their own game, light 'em up!' So me 'n ole Charlie Sphinx, we take out our acetylene torches, and boy, did we ever light up that shaft! We scorched 'em 'n scaled the cable, took possession of the elevator 'n sent the miserable stragglers to China!"

–"They just don't play DENT like that anymore, do they, Bobby!"

–"I'll say, Biff!"

–"For the benefit of our home-viewers, what would you tell them to watch for today?"

–"Look into the eyes of the captain! If he's got that reckless grin, like he'll stop at nothing, he's a winner!"

–"You heard it from Dr. DENT! Join us now as the 159th Floor Spiders take on the Climbers from the 157th! Stay tuned and stand tall!"

3.

Elgin crawled out from behind the overturned bench. He hadn't eaten a crumb since leaving his home cube and now felt a gnawing hunger in his gut. Guided only by instinct in the dark, he had no other recourse but to seek out the archies' position and surprise them before they surprised him. Careful to slip under the heat-sensitive security wires with which they'd cordoned off the dig, he calculated the location of their camp by the gaps in between poles. Archies always lay in wait like spiders, prepared to pounce on any life form that wandered into their web. Elgin crawled up so close he could smell the sweat of a snoring guard. He paused and listened intently to the darkness, detecting nothing but the patter of rats. The archies had foolishly left only a single man behind to guard the dig. Good. Elgin reached his hand out and shuddered when his fingertips grazed the bristles of the sleeping man's beard. The guard grunted in his sleep, no doubt thinking he was shooing away a nosy rodent, and was soon snoring again. Again, Elgin reached his hand out, and this time he struck pay dirt, grasping in turn a spool of alarm wire, a pair of pliers and a high power torch. Elgin pocketed the torch, clipped off two arm-lengths of wire and made a loop. Survival called for swift action. No time for remorse. He lunged forward in the direction of the beard bristles, slipped the curl of wire down over the unsuspecting chin, and when he felt the wire's downwards path interrupted by a bobbing Adam's apple, he yanked it tight. Soon the squirming stopped and Elgin risked turning on his torchlight.

The man lay still. At his feet, rats were battling it out over the remains of his freeze-dried dinner. Elgin scattered the rats with a few well-aimed bits of debris and scooped up the few remaining mouthfuls of turkey, mashed potatoes and peas.—"Don't worry, fellahs," Elgin whispered, stripping the dead man of his gear, "I'll leave you the left-overs."

The thing he had done altered his life forever. His fingertips tingled and he dropped the wire like it was charged. He broke out in a cold sweat. The smell of it repelled him at first. The smell of fear spiked with the smell of excitement and something else. He could feel it too from head to toe. It was like he had burst the confines of his old self, slipped out of his tight-fitting kid skin and left it lying there on the ground of the dig. He peered at his hands like they belonged to someone else. It was as if with a tug of the wire he had instantaneously undergone the desensitivity training his mother had hoped to spare him. He peered at the motionless body that lay there like a misshapen shadow. Is that what it meant to get horizontal? There was no going back now.

In that long night of waiting, Elgin had grown from a troubled boy to a desperate young man. But there was no time to waste on sentimental regrets. Soon enough the uptime crew would be back. They'd find the remains of their fallen comrade and be on his trail pronto. He had to make it to the tunnel.

Elgin shone his torchlight in all directions, till finally he located the faded sign for T ACK 21, where he had twice seen old Cornelius scurry for safety, the first time dissolving in the dark, the second time disintegrating in a flash of light. Without giving it a second thought, Elgin bounded down the rusty track.

4.

Finding the freight elevator unresponsive to repeated signal bells, confirming her suspicions of her son's escape route, Mrs. Marble turned and nodded at Dr. Orion.

PETER WORTSMAN

"That a girl, Elly!" he patted her head.

Revolted by his touch, she willed a prompt reply, activating the ingredients in the pill he'd swallowed, making him double over in a spasm of pain that flashed back and forth between his groin and his kidneys.—"Just a little reminder of the terms of our agreement!" she smiled. "Oh, and please do call me Mrs. Marble!"

It was no trouble at all for the wife of an elevator man who'd taken her along on many a run, romancing her in freefall when they were young, "to tame the mustang," as they said in the vertical trade, and saddle a malfunctioning freight.

*

Monitoring the scene, IVT was ready.

"The fish are biting!" Agent Belfry remarked.

Quirt grinned: "Pity the worm!"

5.

"The boy, he bopped me from behind, honest, Ms. Marble!" Otis assured her, while eying the principal, demonstratively stroking the back of his head. "I took him along on a freight run, let him take the throttle, you know, for old time's sake!"

"Nobody's blaming you, Otis!" Mrs. Marble reassured him, "we just want to find Elgin."

Noting the crooked bespectacled look of the un-smiling bureaucrat, the old freight man sought some assurance of his immunity.—"Honest, if I'd know'd he was up to no good, I'd never'a let him climb into my box! A man don't go courting trouble."

"There's trouble and there's *TROUBLE!*" Dr. Orion smiled with practiced intimidation. "Your cooperation would go a long way to—how shall I put it?—counterbalance any suspicion of culpability."

Increasingly wary, Otis sought reassurance in the familiar face of his old partner's widow: "He was like a son to me, him being Upton's boy. I never figured he'd double-cross me when my back was turned!"

"It's not like Elgin!" she shook her head.

"No, it ain't!" Otis agreed.

"Where was he headed?!" Dr. Orion demanded impatiently.

"I got one set of eyes, Mister," said Otis, "and they ain't located where I part my hair! Somebody bops you from behind, knocks you out cold, you don't know which way is up!"

"Listen, Otis," she grabbed his hand, "Elgin may be in big trouble. You've got to help us find him!"

Otis squinted in the man's direction.

"Dr. Orion is on our side…for now!" she assured

him.

He looked his old partner's wife full in the face, weighing loyalty against prudence, blinking with fear for his own skin and concern for the boy, filtering the truth through his cracked front teeth: "First he tells me he's headed for the artificial nature sanctuary down on Sub-Sub-17. Some kind of story about going rock digging with his archo class next week and wanting to be prepared. Hell, I didn't believe a word of it, Miss Marble, but I wa'n't about to turn him in for playing hooky neither. Even good boys's got a little bad in 'em!" he shrugged.

Dr. Orion screwed his gaze to two burning laser beams: "Aiding and abetting the horizontal escapades of minors is a serious infraction, Mr...."

–"Up, Otis Up, Sir! I ain't abetted nobody! Next thing I know, the boy is asking me to let him out at Sub-Sub-11."

The mother and the principal exchanged telling looks.

–"Not without no authorization disc, I says. No a.d., no exit! That's what I told him. Well wouldn't ya know it? Soon as my back is turned, he goes 'n grabs a monkeywrench, 'n blam! He got his authorization, he did!" Otis demonstratively rubbed the back of his head. "I ain't sayin' I know where's he's headed, but if I was you," he nodded at Mrs. Marble, "I'd look for him down on Sub-Sub-11. They're diggin' down there, that much I know, some kind o' ole station or somethin'. Never been there myself!" he assured the man with the spectacles, "I just haul their gear up and down for them, and the rubble they bring back, that's all. And I don't ask no questions neither. Maybe Elgin's gone scavenging for trinkets. It's bad, I know, but the boy don't mean no harm."

"Take us to Sub-Sub-11!" the principal commanded.

"You got the proper authorization?" Otis asked.

"Please!" Mrs. Marble squeezed his control hand.

6.

The Climbers were gaining on the Spiders. Bravely leading his team, Herbert, Jr. sacrificed two drones to pierce the opposition's synthetic web. "Victory demands selective sacrifice!" his father had always told him. "Let your opponent think you're foolhardy, and while he's gloating you close in for the kill." The Climbers had barbs in their boots and hooks in their gloves that made the ascent easy. The Spiders depended on power scythes and sticky fiber which their advance guards sprayed down the shaft, allowing them to leap boldly into the void, landing on and selectively piercing their own webbing, while immobilizing their opponents long enough for the rear guard to finish them off. In their feeding frenzy, the Spiders had miscalculated the Climbers' upward mobility. Woe betide a careless Spider who leapt into the Climbers' clutches. Before he knew it, he'd be enveloped, first by his feet, then by his torso, and finally head and all, by an indissoluble plastic bubble in which, while watching the match, like a silent film, through the rainbow-colored gossamer bulge, he'd slowly suffocate.

Herbert, Jr. led a daredevil charge up the middle of the pierced web. Most of his men got through, easily overtaking the surprised Spiders, soon enough boarding the elevator, and following a brief scuffle with a few rear guards, piloting the box to victory on the 157th Floor. Alas, Gladys had to look with horror at her Inter-Eye screen as the defeated Spider captain, who'd clung to the bottom of the box, overtook her brave Herbert, Jr. from behind, stung him in the spine and squirted mace into his eyes, whereupon, forestalling the humiliation of defeat, he himself let out a whoop and leapt into the bottomless void.

*

At the victory celebration that followed in the joyous Loyola living cube, Herbert, Sr. toasted his son's team's valiant triumph, as Herbert, Jr., eyes bandaged up and paralyzed though he was, basked in the glory, while his mother fed him forkfuls of the victory cake.

"That's my boy! That's my boy!" Herbert, Sr. kept repeating with a proud paternal grin.

*

–"What a match!"

–"I'll say! It's a great day for the 157th Floor Climbers."

–"Their captain got a little roughed up, though, didn't he?"

"Rough 'n tumble's the name of the game!" Bobby beamed, slapping Biff on the back. "It's the spice of the sport. DENT wouldn't be DENT without it."

"You bet!" said Biff.

7.

There's always a light at the end of the tunnel. Elgin kept whispering the old lie to himself as he cut loose down the track, and stumbling on a loose cross-tie, picked himself up again and kept running. It may be a thousand miles, but I'm gonna make it! he played cheerleader to a fading dream. But the fading torchlight turned up nothing but track and tunnel. The air got thinner and thinner and Elgin soon felt winded. His pace slowed from a sprint to a stride to a determined stumble. What's the use? he muttered, collapsing onto the track, switching his light off to preserve the battery. Elgin rubbed his cheek against the cold rusty metal. And just when he was about to give up all hope of ever reaching anywhere but the suffocating here and now, he felt faint vibrations rippling through the metal. Little by little, the vibrations swelled into a sound, at first indistinct, but as he pressed his ear hard against the rail, the sound increased in volume and clarity. No doubt about it, it was the clatter and scrape of metal on metal, the sound of something moving toward him in the dark. Switching on his torchlight, Elgin held his feeble breath, as a handcar braked inches short of his skull.

At the handle stood a man whom Elgin immediately recognized as the derelict from Block 367789.

"That was pretty dumb!" the man shook his head.

–"You might have been IVT."

"You might have been pulverized! Here, put this on and take a deep breath!" he said, handing the boy an oxygen mask. "All aboard!" he cried to a nonexistent platform full of passengers, his voice echoing in the dark. Elgin climbed aboard and, as soon as the derelict pumped the handcar into motion, drifted off to sleep.

8.

"My head is a coconut," the man said, "every morning I crack it and milk it."

–"Isn't there an easier way?"

"I could break off an arm," he reflected, "but it's not likely to grow back quickly in this thin atmosphere."

His cellmate was pounding his head against the stone wall. Was this the 13th Floor?

Then he heard crying. "Is there a baby in this place?"

Now the cell was an elevator sinking and there was no one to answer his question.

"Look inside!" a voice said.

Shutting his eyes, he found to his amazement, that a reflective slime on the insides of his eyelids made them function like parallel mirrors. In their reflection he saw himself simultaneously at different ages, one self inside the shell of another.

"Scrambled egghead!" the voice jeered.

"I want out!" Elgin screamed.

"So do we all!" his simultaneous selves shrieked in unison, as Elgin awakened from troubled sleep.

*

PETER WORTSMAN

"You hungry? Would you like reconstituted eggs?" asked the derelict from Block 367789.

The lighting was artificial, as were the bird sounds. But a real stream of water flowed from one seemingly impenetrable cave wall to another. Vegetation of various species and dimensions, from shrub to brush to sapling, lined the banks.

"Is this the Great Outdoors?" Elgin asked, searching for the fabled stars in the overhanging rock.

"I'm afraid not," the man smiled, "but we hope to get to space someday."

–"*We?*"

–"Us Crabs."

–"So you do exist!"

"Pincers and all," the man laughed, displaying a long metal pole with a mechanical clasp at the end, with which he reached up to the topmost branches of a fairly tall tree and retrieved a round red object.— "Have an apple!"

It was the first fresh apple Elgin had ever tasted and he savored each bite, licking the sweet trickle that dripped down the sides of his mouth. He bit and chewed more slowly now, wanting the sensations to last, when a sudden gurgling sound supplanted the pleasure he took in the taste and texture of the fruit. Bubbles rose from the river, followed by the head of a creature with a spout protruding upwards, dragging a big fish behind. Elgin leapt back in terror. Crawling ashore, the big-boned amphibian removed its facemask and shook loose its hair and proved to be a female of human features.

–"Where did you dig *him* up?"

–"Nearly ran him over with the hand car."

–"How do you know he isn't IVT?"

–"He's a friend, saved me from the block patrol."

With a sucking sound, she pealed off the rubber sheath.

Elgin stared at her angular nakedness.

"Hand me a rag, will you!" she laughed.

Laughing in turn, the man flung her a cloth, with which she wiped her long black hair, making no effort to cover herself.

Her eyes were black and curved at the corners, unlike any Elgin had ever seen on his block, and he could not take his own eyes off them or the rest of her.

"What is she?" he asked the man.

–"Ask her, she won't bite!"

"Which block do you belong to?" Elgin timidly inquired, his gaze taking refuge at her toes.

"I'm from the other side," she said.

–"The other side of what?"

PETER WORTSMAN

"China," she smiled.

"But I thought…!" Elgin tried to imagine her upside-down.

Reading his confusion, she leapt into the air and landed on her hands.—"How do you do?" she said, extending the dripping wet big toe of her right foot.

Landing back on her feet, she and the man laughed heartily, and Elgin cracked a hesitant smile, taking fleeting peaks at the tuft of hair between her legs, from which drops of water ran down.

V

1.

They were gathered round a crude table rock that the river had cut out. The old man groped for a gourd of water, knocking it over in the process.

"While the young go on digging," he said, "we old ones are content to dig inwards. Mind tunnels run deep!" It was the second time Elgin had heard mention of such a thing, the first time from the lips of the derelict from Block 367789, who smiled at him now from across the table. "Some of you despair too easily. You say we will never emerge from bare rock, that the digging is futile. Some have left our ranks and returned to the verticals. Go in peace! I tell you. Who knows? Perhaps the outside is indeed more cherished dream than tangible reality, since no one alive has actually ever seen so much as a flicker of sunlight. Or perhaps it is a terrible place, desolate, uninhabitable, devoid of life, as they pretend. And only the inside is safe. But in digging out, we continue to encounter others, poor deluded fools, every bit as determined and desperate as ourselves, and so we grow our ranks and swell the labyrinth of possibility. But I tell you, my friends, only when your hands are as calloused and your knuckles as gnarled from digging as mine"—he spread his fingers wide and held them aloft—"only when you've despaired of ever actually breaking through does the doubt harden into a helmet and shield and the real battle begin."

Whereupon the old man lowered his head and all those gathered round the table raised the carcass of the big fish they'd devoured, the one the woman had caught in the underground river, gnawed to the bone, and solemnly repeated after him, reciting in unison:

"In the bone we see the sky,

A retrospective landscape.

Let the sun die a soft escape,

And the eye be reduced to an image,

No angel fallen, but a fact reflected,

Wistful upon the where."

2.

"I'm Park, this is Meadow," the derelict from Block 367789 introduced himself and his companion, the woman who had emerged from the water.

–"Elgin Marble, how do you do!"

"How do we know he's clean?" a redheaded man scowled at Elgin.

"We'll give him a bath!" Meadow scoffed, setting off a burst of laughter around the table. Elgin laughed too. Meadow's easygoing way was infectious. He kept replaying in his mind's eye the sight of her emerging from the water, peeling off her rubber sheath, then leaping onto her hands and reaching her big toe out for him to shake. Each individual was dressed in clothes of their own confection, some haphazardly stitched together, some skillfully tailored. Meadow wore a dress with a flower pattern that hugged her hips. Elgin waited till she turned away to cast a fleeting look of longing in her direction.

"What if he's IVT!?" the redhead challenged.

"Well, *are* you?" Meadow once again took Elgin by surprise with a disarming smile.

Elgin blushed.

"The boy's clean!" said Park.

"What's the basis of your prognosis?" the redhead fired back with an unvarnished hint of hostility.

–"Instinct, Field! The same sense that makes my skin crawl whenever I think of you!"

"Please! Please!" the old man held up his hands. "Even if the boy were IVT, they'd have to have planted sonar bugs under his skin and nano-radar in his nose for him to be of any use to them. In which case, the damage is already done and they have our precise whereabouts pegged and are listening and closing in at this very moment. But I am inclined to trust Park's instinct. What is the view of the majority?"

A general consensus favored Elgin's acceptance.

"I'll bow to the will of the majority," Field conceded, still defiant, "but that doesn't mean I won't keep an eye on him. We've worked too hard for too long to let sentiment jeopardize our operation!"

"You talk like we were terrorists living up to our IVT profile!" the old man reproached him.

–"Well aren't we!? Don't we stand for their collapse!"

The old man shook his head. "Let them live as they like, so long as they let us do likewise, and who knows, maybe one day our intentions will meet."

"With all due respect, Yosemite," Field barely contained his fury, "the vertical order is anathema to our very existence, and you know it. If only the scattered Crab beds were united in a common struggle, we might stand a chance against them."

"I can't stop you," Yosemite sighed, " and from a strategic standpoint, no doubt you are right. But I cannot help but fear that in banding together, as you put it, our free horizontal urge would soon harden into a credo every bit as oppressive as that of the vertical world we escaped. Remember that their ancient symbol of suffering, to which they only still give lip service, consists of vertical and horizontal links."

"It's all a game of tic-tac-toe to you, cruci-fact or

-fiction!" Field replied with a self-satisfied sarcastic grin.

Meanwhile Park winked at Meadow, who took Elgin by the hand and the three slipped away unnoticed.

3.

"We come from various blocks and sectors," Park talked as they walked, pausing every now and then to point out the outlay of the labyrinthine linked caverns. "Our talents are as varied as our origins. Take Wuppertal there, for instance," he said, pointing to a white-haired man with almost translucent skin who stood stooped over on a rickety scaffolding clearly of his own construction, the open palms of his hands pressed against the rock, with hand-drill, paint brushes, and other tools and utensils piled in a heap at his feet. "He's been at it for as far back as anyone can remember. Without him, I'm afraid, we'd have all long since succumbed to the claustrophobia of life underground and gone completely mad. Not inclined to talk while he's working, he doesn't mind others admiring his handiwork. Let's have a look."

Elgin turned his attention to the tube-like passageway in which they now found themselves. The walls were covered with intricate murals, some of recognizable scenes, others depicting nothing but the colors and shapes they seemed to be celebrating with wild abandon.

"When Wuppertal first broke through," Park continued, "he hugged the bare rock around him. IVT had kept him locked up in a tiny cell hardly large enough for him to stand up in, let alone roll over."

"What was his crime?" Elgin asked.

"Horizontal leanings, like the rest of us," Park shrugged. "He spent the endless temporal span of his incarceration decorating his cell. It amused his keepers and kept him quiet, so they let him have a hand-drill, brushes and paint." Some even found themselves included in the mural with a smug grin and a patronizing hand on his shoulder. Flattered, indignant, they liked to taunt him: 'Hey, Wuppertal, maybe one day you'll paint yourself a woman or a window!' And then one day he did. He was painting and drilling, drilling and painting. One moment, he recalled, he was in the cell, and the next moment he was…elsewhere."

Elgin and Park paused to admire the three-dimensional depiction of a massive tower reaching up into the rock clouds, with workmen scurrying about like ants.

"That's Babel, the first skyscraper," Park explained. "which is where things started to go wrong."

Beside it Elgin noticed a soaring edifice with a big monkey hugging its pointed spire.—"Isn't that the Empire State Building? I've got a friend named after it."

"That's right," Park nodded. "And there," he pointed at two identical towers in flames, "are the fabled…"

"World Trade Center!" Elgin finished the sentence with a schoolboy's excitement.

"You get an A in vertical aptitude!" Park clapped a hand on his shoulder.

–"Ugh! Don't remind me!"

"You know," said Park, "I used to be a teacher."

Remembering how and where they met, with Park laid out flat out on the floor, Elgin cracked a smile: "You're pulling my leg!"

"No, really," Park insisted, "though I had a certain tendency to toy with the acceptable parameters, which rubbed some of my colleagues, and especially my superiors, the wrong way."

"Praised be the Pyramid of Progress," Elgin rattled off from memory, tilting the flat palms of his hands over his head in a symbolic triangle, his elbows extended to complete the base. "The future rests on the foundation of our efforts!" he declaimed with mock reverence.

"Bravo, my boy, you learned your lesson well!"

Park conferred a lapsed pedagogue's approval. "But what about the inverted pyramid of yesterday's present or the shapeless prospect of tomorrow? There's wisdom lost in what we trample underfoot or fail to imagine! Word of my 'subverted geometry,' as they called it, reached the board of education. They recommended a respite from student contact and reassigned me to the archives. A definite mistake, from their perspective, as the electronic files I pored over merely fueled—what's the right term?—'latent horizontal leanings' and a shameless scorn for…"

"The ineluctable climb of mankind!" Elgin filled in the blanks with a wink.

"And now for the extra credit question,"—Park clearly still liked teaching—"identify all the famous edifices in this image in less than thirty seconds and you get a falling star."

Racing along, Elgin shouted out the names of the historical heights he recognized: "Tree of Life…Mount Everest…Calvary…the Pyramids…Chrysler Building…Eiffel Tower…Leaning Tower of Pisa…Washington Monument…Hancock Building…Tower of London…Cleopatra's Needle…Alpha Obelisk…Qtar Ski slope…" He stopped short in front of a tall blue-green emanation, part tower, part tree, sprouting branches and piercing the sky, with a naked couple looking up from the topmost branch and a child waving down from the clouds.— "What's that?"

–"Wuppertal won't tell! Some call it Jack and the Beanstalk, some Adam and Eve up a tree. I call it Wuppertal's wet dream."

Staring at the naked woman in the mural, Elgin thought of Meadow, feeling a tingle and a rise.

4.

"Betrayal," said Dr. Orion, "is in the nature of the beast." The old freight elevator sank slowly, rattling and creaking as it dropped. The principal killed time by expounding his personal philosophy. He liked to hear himself speak. "Let's be perfectly frank, my dear, we all have a price. Mine is ambition. Yours is your boy. His welfare is of paramount importance. We'd both do anything to find him, which makes us companions in crime."

–"Shut up, Orion!"

–"Naturally, I understand your feelings toward me, and honestly, I don't blame you. You despise me, though I for my part did derive a considerable amount of pleasure from our little…get-acquainted session? You spoke of loneliness. I, too, am a lonely man."

–"Save it for your next horizon parlor visit, honey!"

"Dear lady,"—Dr. Orion inched closer to her as

they sank, feeling the downward thrust of the elevator in his loins—"destiny has placed us in close proximity on a common mission. Who knows how long it will take or if we ever come up again? We might as well make the best of our time together," he said, slinging an arm around her shoulder and another round her waist.

"Down boy!" She willed another spasm of pain in his scrotum that made him sink to his knees. "From my mind to your testicles! My shoes need shining, perhaps you could oblige with a spit polish." Trembling, he licked them from heel to toe. "Good boy!" she patted his bald head.

Keeping a mental countdown of the psycho-suggestion pill's 24-hour duration, he cringed, his scrotum still smarting. And yet, he took a certain twisted pleasure in such crude debasement, far better than the contrived effects of any horizon parlor. She was a real pro and at least her hatred was true. No stronger emotion had ever been directed at him. And for the first time in his life, for a fleeting instant, Dr. Orion was truly moved.

5.

He was a jealous Jack dangling like a human string bean from Wuppertal's magic beanstalk, peering down at Park and Meadow playing Adam and

Eve—or was it his father and mother?—lying in naked embrace. "I want to play too!" he cried out and tried to slide down the beanstalk. But the farther he fell, the faster and taller it grew. Despairing of ever making it all the way down, he let go and jumped.

"Wake up, little man, there's work to be done!" A voice sounded at once in the distance and in the extreme proximity of a dream.

Elgin opened his eyes, deeply embarrassed. "Boys will be boys!" Meadow laughed, turned her back and flung him a rag to clean himself off. "Park's off on one of his scouting missions. Every time that man leaves the domestic circle, I'm afraid I'll never see him again. Sometimes I think he's addicted to danger. It's my own fault for getting tangled up with a Crab!" She pretended to shrug off her fear, though Elgin could sense it. "I've taken the morning off from my duties to help you get acclimatized to freedom. It won't be easy at first. What did you used to do in downtime, young man?"

–"Nothing much."

–"Could you be a bit more specific?"

–"I foraged."

–"What for?"

–"Antiquities."

–"Oh?"

–"Tickets was my thing."

–"A ticket taker, now there's a useful pursuit with nowhere to go!"

–"Tickets to places, dream destinations."

"Don't mind me," she winked, "I'm a tease."

"I'm thick-skinned," he lied.

"As I can see," she called his bluff. "When I was a girl, believe it or not, I dreamed of camping out in the W.C. It was the only place I could be alone. And I liked the sound of rushing water!" she laughed.

"That's funny," Elgin flashed back to the girl in the school bathroom, but kept the association to himself.

–"I didn't much like school, you see, so when it came time to pick a job I thought, why not be a diver for the water works. You had to be pretty slender to fit through the conduits and I was skinny as a twig. We were sent out to check on leaks and to detect potential weak spots in the re-channeled underground Yangtze river system. The drainage pipes were red, the fresh water main was green. One day there was a really tough job, the kind of job that involved a certain risk, and for which they gave you a six-hour air supply, instead of the standard three, and an extra sack of rice. I and another girl volunteered. They never sent us out alone. The current was strong. You generally just let it carry you to the problem spot, where you switched on your electromagnetic harness, and stuck fast to the pipe wall until the job was done. Then they deflected the flow just long enough for you to climb through a nearby lock and up through a manhole. Tiananmen floated on ahead. She waved to signal an imminent braking. I waved back to acknowledge her signal, but a strange and powerful urge suddenly came over me: What if I just kept going!? Waving wildly, watching me glide by, she was helpless to stop me. It felt so wonderful to glide along, to go with the flow wherever it might take me. So what if my air supply gave out and I drowned, at least I'd die free. Park found me and fished me out of a drainage basin on one of his long distance reconnaissance missions. Who knows how long I'd been floating there unconscious. It was all so dreamlike. We've been practicing mouth-to-mouth resuscitation ever since."

Elgin imagined himself in Park's place, knee-deep in the stream, his mouth pressed to hers.

"Come along!" she said. "Yosemite is waiting."

6.

The old man made a show of fluttering his nostrils and cocking his ears. "Meadow, and our new arrival, welcome!" he smiled, rising to greet them, "I may be blind, but I can still appreciate a woman's scent."

"Yosemite, please," she smiled back, "think of the example you're setting for the boy!"

–"I *am*, my dear, I assure you. Adolescence and senility have a few things in common. The longing's the same, the fumbling too, only the perspective is different: he's looking forward, I'm looking back."

"While his raging hormones can still be reined in," Meadow kept up the merry patter, "we ought to find him some socially useful form of sublimation."

"What does he like?" Yosemite inquired.

–"Antiquities."

–"A dealer?"

–"He specializes in tickets to nowhere."

–"At the moment I'm afraid the infrequency of arrivals and departures here hardly merits a ticket taker. It's the slow season!"

"When has it ever been busy?" Meadow grinned.

Yosemite shook his head with mock concern.— "Perhaps we ought to advertise on Inter-Eye to attract the vertical tourist trade."

"Excellent idea," she concurred, "though I'm sure they already simulate Crab tours in select horizon parlors!"

"Leave us, Meadow, before I forget my age and blindness," Yosemite winked, "the boy and I have much to talk about."

VI

1.

"Let me warn you," the old man placed a hand on the boy's shoulder, "I don't always tell the truth, but if you listen carefully, you'll learn to pick out the fraudulent vibrations."

"But how do you get by," Elgin hesitated, "without eyes, I mean?"

"Here," said Yosemite, removing a rag he kept tied around his neck, revealing a nasty scar, "take it and wrap it tightly around your eyes."

The boy pretended to do as the old man said, binding the cloth loosely enough so that he could still peak out the bottom.

"What do you see?" Yosemite asked.

"Nothing," Elgin lied.

"Your nothing's full of holes," the old man laughed. "Lying is an art, my boy. You'll have to do better than that or else make do with the truth."

Smiling to himself, Elgin tied the cloth tightly.

"Better let me lead," Yosemite took the first step forward. "I'm more practiced at blindness and deceit."

Greeting the first person they passed, Yosemite called out his name before the latter had uttered a word.—"Still fooling with the fillies, Fjord, you old fool?"

"Just what I was going to ask you, Yosemite, you dirty old philanderer," Fjord replied, "the boy's not exactly your type!"

Yosemite shrugged. "At our age, you take what you can get!"

The two old men exchanged a hearty laugh.

"Come along, my boy, we'd best keep our distance," Yosemite counseled, "his bite is much worse than his bark!"

"At least I've still got my teeth!" Fjord called after them.

They kept on walking.

Stumbling at first, Elgin saw with his feet. "You weren't born blind, were you?" he blurted out.

"20-20 in hindsight," Yosemite nodded, "surgeons need a modicum of skill."

"A surgeon?" the boy stopped dead in his tracks. "We learned about them in school, how they used to cut people open to tinker with the ticker and take out all kinds of nasty stuff. I thought they became obsolete in the 21st century."

"Indeed they did," Yosemite confessed, "except on the 13th Floor!"

Elgin shuddered.

"A job's a job," the old man shrugged. "Specialized in experimental transplants, I did my job and asked no questions till I made a little mistake. Gave a faulty human thumper to a baboon and the monkey's infallible muscle to the man. The human turned out well enough, all things considered, but the baboon lost his heart to the female gorilla in the next cage over."

–"You're pulling my leg!"

–"I'm serious!"

Caught between a grin, a grimace and a wince, Elgin didn't know what to do with his face.

"Stem cells are cleaner than scalpels," Yosemite said. "You can grow back a severed hand or even a pair of beating ventricles, but you can't stimulate the return of love once it's lost. 'I'd see more of you if I had a piece of me missing!' my wife complained, but I didn't listen. Then one day she up and left me. Even baboons' hearts break."

–"But what about your eyes?"

–"An accident, or perhaps it was deliberate."

–"You always speak in riddles."

"It's all a big riddle, boy: Where do *I* end and *you* begin? We shed odors and vibrations like snakes shed their skin." Yosemite paused. "You might as well walk along with us, Field, the acoustics are better up close!"

Lifting the rag, Elgin spotted the silent stalker

trailing close behind.

"Just checking in," Field tried to fake levity. "How's our young friend doing?"

Yosemite turned to Elgin. "Let me introduce our self-appointed security chief!"

–"We've already met."

–"Field was low-level IVT on the other side, for which sin he has forever been expiating."

"Sometimes," said Field, "it feels like I'm protecting you fools from yourselves!"

"For which we are forever beholden," Yosemite bowed his head.

Field held the smile. "I don't suppose the good doctor told you how he made his escape?"

"Walked through the looking glass, more than likely," Elgin laughed.

"Not quite!" The merriment suddenly drained from Field's face, though the telling clearly gave him pleasure. "His disappearance was a great mystery until I cracked it. Let me enlighten you, since I was the agent in charge of the case. Disease having been eradicated and the ever burgeoning population threatening to eat up the planet, medicine was put to alternative uses, for prophylaxis and selection, shall we say. The good doctor engaged in certain unsavory scientific studies for the Institute." And turning to Yosemite: "Or did you withhold that piece of the puzzle?"

Yosemite said nothing.

"A few minor mishaps, missing organs and such, and a little dillydallying with sedated patients proved an embarrassment to his superiors. Very unscientific! Downright diagonal! A public scandal loomed." Field continued. "Conscience stricken, the doctor hatched an exit plan. With the aid of a doting nurse, he had himself sewn inside the skin of a gorilla he himself had inseminated, a bloated pregnant female, whose fetus, uterus and everything else he removed to make room. The doctor donned a wet suit and installed an elastic cord and magnetic anchor in place of the ape's intestinal tract, to be shot out the anal sphincter and vagina, so as to stall his host body's descent down the old ODC long enough for the doctor to climb out on Sub-Sub-11 and escape to this very Crab encampment."

"Repulsive!" Yosemite cringed. "You IVT people have a positively pornographic imagination!"

"Ex-IVT!" Field corrected. "I spent so much time studying his case, he got under my skin. Never did report the escape route. Instead, I paid him the ultimate tribute. I followed in his footsteps."

"Is it true?!" Elgin asked Yosemite.

−"What do you think?"

Elgin thought he smelled a lie.

"Oh, and by the way," Field added, "he isn't a hundred percent blind either, just a little fuzzy eyed."

2.

Dr. Orion bent over the body of the dead archeologist, whose vacant gaze was fixed on the starry firmament overhead.

Mrs. Marble shook her head: "I just don't believe Elgin could have done such a thing! Not the Elgin I know!"

"That's just it, Mrs. Marble," he said. "Let me try to put this as delicately as I can. What if…he's not the Elgin you know? Adolescence is a time of flux. A period of dangerous hormonal imbalance. Previously docile obedient boys give vent to violent outbursts. That's why desensitization is so essential!" He talked like a text tape.

"Elgin! Elgin!" Mrs. Marble cried out, all the fear and longing encapsulated into that one word reverberating against the great domed ceiling. "We want to help you!"

"HELP YOU!…HELP YOU!" the ceiling mocked her tears.

"Was this a sanctuary?" she shuddered.

"A train station," Dr. Orion shared her dread. He bent down and picked up a shred of pounded wood pulp, reading aloud: "'FEDERAL TRANSIT AID INTENDED TO EASE THE CRUSH.'"

The wide open space and the proximity of the woman for whom he had such mixed sentiments—and to whom he was pharmacologically attached—made him anxious. To hide his malaise and try to fill the emptiness he reverted to pedagogical mode. Once he got started, he couldn't stop himself.

"Things got so bad, I understand," he expounded, "that people were regularly crushed to death at downtime by the mass of commuters fighting to squeeze into the trains to the outlying districts. That's when the first vertical laws were enacted, restricting nonessential displacement. Outdated building statutes were modified to allow for taller and taller skyscrapers. Foundations were fortified and expanded. Cities spread. But still the desperate swarmed to the ever more distant suburbs. Finally, all traffic was outlawed and the ramps themselves—highways they called them—were filled in and built up by visionary urban planners, undoing the damage of their predecessors. The rivers were rerouted underground and the riverbeds drained to make room. Landfills stretched farther and farther out into the vast salt water basins, colossal fish tanks were built to breed fish, and eventually the sea itself was filled in. These old stations were left to the elements, but pressing spatial needs soon encroached on any lingering nostalgia for an outmoded past.

Then came The Great Disruption, followed by the mad dash for space settlements and the building boom of the 22nd-century. The rubble of the past was ploughed under, and layer upon layer, we built up our beautiful vertical world. 'The sky's the limit!' they used to say, until the phrase became as archaic as the notion."

"Shut up!" she said, preferring silence. Mrs. Marble peered long and hard at the painted sky, blackened where the fire had devoured the paint and the stone reasserted itself. She remembered from childhood a school visit to a planetarium, where a light show approximated a virtual reconstitution of the heavens, based on the primitive records and calculations of 21st-century astronomers, the last humans to have actually seen it, but the planetariums had long since been demolished to make way for needed living space.

"Just think of it, Mrs. Marble!" Dr. Orion solemnly declared, ignoring her upset, awed by the implications of his own words. "Mankind's dominion of the universe has only just begun. Together, you and I, and Elgin, too, once he comes to his senses, could play our own small part in helping to fill in uselessly empty space and forge that future!"

–"Is that a proposal?"

Dr. Orion smiled, well pleased with himself, certain that his words had made a deep and lasting impression and that he had finally won her over. And just as he was about to plant a calculated kiss on Mrs. Marble's lips, already relishing the liberties he might now take with impunity—not that he planned to marry her, just to string her along for his pleasure till the boy was located and taken into custody— the woman, in turn, intended to will a spasm, but a rat beat her to it, leaping out of the rubble, swiftly, as though it had wings, and digging its teeth into his rump, brought the principal back down to earth with a howl of pain. He kicked around him in the dimness of the station, but the rat was indistinguishable from the rubble. "Damn it!" he wailed, any notion of romance faded, "We've got to find that boy!"

3.

As soon as the missing person's face flashed on the screen, Gladys Loyola gasped: "Heavens, it's Elgin! It's Elgin Marble!"

—"We interrupt this transmission to bring you a special report. IVT officers on the case have established conclusively that the missing boy from Block 367790 has been abducted by radical Crabs. Any persons with clues as to the whereabouts of the boy or his abductors are instructed to contact the authorities immediately! Stay tuned and stand tall!"

"It's Ellen's boy! I can't believe it!" Gladys shook

her head, suddenly fathoming why her best friend had missed the big day. "Poor Ellen must be beside herself!"

"For up's sake, Gladys, will you please stop yapping!" Herbert, Sr. barked. "Herbert, Jr. and I want to watch the match."

Decked out, like his Dad, in full DENT regalia, including helmet and shoulder pads, knee caps and crotch guard, himself immobile, strapped into his seat, that doubled as a privy, Herbert, Jr., proved the epitome of manly restraint. His father had to wrap the boy's frozen fingers round his championship trophy.—"That's your trophy, son, you won it and don't you forget it!" All Herbert Jr. could emit was a gurgle in response, which his father interpreted as a rallying cry. And raising his own trophy in the air, the bronze effigy of an elevator man he had won on that proud day twenty some odd years ago, when he himself had led the Climbers to victory, Herbert, Sr. shed and promptly wiped a telltale tear.

"Yes, dear," Gladys responded on cue, but her thoughts were with Ellen. Wavering between sympathy, pity, and a patchwork composite of I-told-you-so, if-only-you'd-listened, you-got-yours, and I-hope-you've-finally-learned-your-lesson,   Gladys kept shaking her head, half convinced that if she shook it enough she could clear the disturbing image from the screen. Affection is, after all, the candy coating of other less laudable emotions.

Peter Wortsman

Ellen had always been the bright and pretty darling of the 159th Floor—which is why Gladys, with a certain innate cunning, sought her out, for to be associated with her was to share in her aura. Gladys was grateful when Ellen let her tag along to floor and later to block activities. And as for Ellen, her own motivation was hardly magnanimity, but rather a reciprocal flustered gratitude that anyone would make such a big fuss over her. And while Ellen readily shared her glamour with Gladys, Gladys helped Ellen get grounded.

Lying side by side on the hydro-massage sofa after school, the two girls giggled, swapping secret dreams of visiting simulated distant places and times, and took turns playing hostess and passenger. Having compared anatomical differences with the boys in the off duty freight elevator, and being the more physically developed and experienced of the two, Gladys coached her friend: "You talk too much!"

But when the boys began to notice the differences, they invariably did their fawning over Ellen and their groping with Gladys.

Ellen was always a little distant, as if her mind traveled apart from her body and her thoughts were elsewhere. She could have married into the highest spire of society, Gladys thought back with envy, anger and disenchanted idolatry, on how her friend had wasted her genetic potential. And while Gladys nabbed a brash elevator supervisor, a bulky young man not overly burdened with brains or feelings, but who was definitely going places and didn't mind whom he had to elbow aside to get there, Ellen fell for a common elevator repairman, a gangly young man with an irreverent grin.—"You gotta be kidding, honey, I mean, really!"

Still, inexplicably, Ellen stuck by him. And though Gladys now had her own hands full with Herbert, "a little dense, but very vertical," as she admitted with a girlish titter, it upset her no end to see her old friend drift away. Despite their physical proximity as next-door neighbors—Gladys had arranged things, thanks to Herbert's connections—Ellen was less present than before.

"You save your secrets for Upton now!" she protested, to which Ellen replied with a smile and a shrug, all the more enraging and perplexing Gladys, since she could hardly imagine a conversation of any duration with her husband. "Herbert's not a man of words, thank heavens," she said, to save face, "but boy is he ever up to it! You know what they say: 'Elevator men do it up and down!'"

Then Ellen had Elgin and Gladys had Herbert Jr., and though Ellen declined to join the IVT Ladies Auxiliary, of which Gladys became floor chairlady, the two friends returned to a chatty complicity, comparing notes on casseroles and behavior modification.

PETER WORTSMAN

But as Elgin grew up, Gladys began to notice the same distance in him she'd always felt in Ellen. The boy was bright and polite, but never all there. "He's too internal!" Gladys warned. Elgin was tall, like his father, with the same irreverent grin that made you think he was forever enjoying a private joke at your expense. Gladys pleaded with Ellen to enroll him in the floor DENT team, of which her Herbert Jr. became captain. "It'll straighten out that smirk, knock some sense into him," she said.

"I'll talk to Upton," Ellen replied evasively, invariably deflecting the conversation to her African violets.

Gladys felt badly for her old friend the day Upton got his disposal notice, and yet with a twinge of guilt, refrained from urging Herbert to intercede, secretly hoping it would bring them closer together again. She and her husband went over the downtime before to pay their obligatory respects and say their goodbyes, but when Herbert Sr. got on the subject of duty and solemnly declared that there were two tests in a man's life, moments that called for courage and sacrifice, his DENT match and his disposal, Upton grimaced and Ellen, who had always kept a lid on her emotions in public, asked them to leave. Awkward as it was, Gladys forgave Ellen, knowing what duress she must be under, and dutifully marched beside her, holding her hand at the disposal ceremony, in her dual capacity as IVT

Ladies Auxiliary floor chairlady and lifelong friend.

But a certain formality set in between them after that, a formality Gladys sadly regretted and badly needed to break through the day of Herbert Jr.'s DENT match and victory celebration. She'd felt betrayed that Ellen hadn't been there to stand by and cheer. Now she understood why. Elgin was missing. Crab abduction was the common euphemism for attempted escape, the consequence of which, should the boy be caught, she preferred not to imagine. Again she shook her head to clear the upsetting image. And peering proudly now at her two heroes seated side by side, the pillars of her life, clutching their trophies, the one in an easy chair and the other in a wheelchair, she realized how lucky she was and how badly things had turned out for her friend. "Oh Ellen," she whispered, "if only you'd followed my advice!" And when the DENT match on the Inter-Eye came to its dramatic climax, she could not help but glow with jubilation as Herbert Sr. cheered and Herbert Jr. gurgled.

4.

Meadow dove.

Girded in a second skin, underwater she felt safe. As happy as she was in the caverns among the Crabs, water was still her true element. The way it parts before you like open lips. The way it lets you slip through its embrace, never jealous, always understanding and forgiving. Ground holds back. Water gives.

Every morning Meadow scoured the underground riverbed, letting the current carry her, making mental record of the submerged grottos in the rock, preparing for the inevitable day when the Crabs would be rooted out and forced to flee their present bed and seek another. She often found herself after a while swimming circles around her favorite destination, a massive statue of a woman lying flat on her back with wild irradiated eyes, a spiked crown on her head and one arm extended, either pointing, waving for help, or as Meadow liked to believe, gesturing: Up yours! to the last.

5.

"Better bestir those little legs," Agent Belfry teased his compact colleague, "we've got a date with a mole in the tunnel!"

The mole was already waiting for them, a kerchief wrapped around the face to hide his identity, a sack around the torso to camouflage gender, voice distorted by an oxygen mask.—"You're late!"

–"My partner here had his mind in his pants. He was hoping to hook up with a femme fatale."

–"My falsetto's a little rusty."

–"He'll get over it."

"What about the boy?" Quirt tired of the teasing.

–"A pedophile no less!?"

–"So help me, I'm going to belt him one!"

"He's a little testy, I'm afraid," Belfry shrugged, "The pressures of the job."

–"I sympathize."

–"About the boy?"

–"Vacationing down under."

–"Comfortable lodgings, I trust."

–"Rock-bottom! Speaking of which, I was wondering, with the soaring cost of replacement body parts…!"

Belfry turned gruff: "Cash on delivery."

VII

1.

As Elgin lay curled up in a pleasant daze beside the fire in Park's and Meadow's domestic circle, a winged body flew by overhead carrying something in its beak, accidentally dropping its reluctant lunch on the boy's leg, where it settled and likewise curled up. And when the disgruntled winged thing came swooping back to retrieve its prey, the boy instinctively cupped his hand and curled his fingers protectively around the worm, as if it were a part of him, catching a nasty scratch from an angry beak. Uncurling his fingers, he found, to his horror, that he had squeezed so hard he'd crushed it, now a lifeless ooze, in the palm of his hand. He rubbed it off on his leg and licked the bloody scratch, grabbing a rock from the ground, prepared to fight off the flying offender, but laughter followed instead of the expected squawk.

A honey-colored girl about his own age with a round halo of hair leapt out from behind a nearby bolder, the laughter still spewing like a geyser from her lips. Feeling deeply embarrassed, and oddly thrilled, as if he'd been caught with his pants down and did not really mind it, Elgin hid behind a mask of anger: "What's so funny?!"

–"Don't you believe in laughter?"

–"Not if I'm the butt of it."

"I dreamt of you," the girl giggled, "we were freefalling down an elevator shaft and neither of us could find the emergency button."

–"What happened?"

–"I woke up."

–"How long have you been watching me?"

–"A while."

–"Why?"

–"Just curious, I guess. They said you were tall and…"

–"And?"

–"Gawky looking."

–"Thanks for the compliment."

–"What's it like going up and down?"

Now it was Elgin's turn to laugh and the girl's turn to be cross.

–"It's funny, that's all."

–"What's funny?"

–"We've got inverted dreams. All my life I've wanted to break out, and the first freeborn horizontal I meet dreams of going up and down.

This time they both laughed.

"I'm Elgin," he held out his hand.

"Equator," she winked and took off without warning, barefoot but nimble, across the rocky pathway through the circuit of caves.

2.

"One move and you'll be an instant artifact!" said the archeologist who materialized little by little in the afterglow of the blinding high-intensity beam, one hand holding the torch, the other gripping an eliminator. Another archeologist stood by, likewise armed.

"I can't tell you how glad I am to see you gentlemen!" Dr. Orion affected relief, as if he were merely an innocent bystander or an unwilling party to trespass in the forbidden zone.

"Why bless my soul, it's a talking King Tut!" the taller of the two observed.

"Mummies have been known to disintegrate before your very eyes!" his squat partner grinned.

"Don't waste your batteries!" Mrs. Marble quipped, immediately recognizing the pair of IVT agents who'd paid her an unwelcome visit.

"Nefertiti talks too!" Belfry nodded.

"Since you're so damn talkative, honey," Quirt snarled, shining his light on the strangled archeologist, "maybe you would be so good as to tell us which one of you garroted Big Eyes here!"

"We're on the same side of the law, Officer," the principal piped up, "hunting for clues like yourselves!"

"Which law might that be?" asked Belfry.

–"Same law that puts eliminators in the hands of gangsters and clowns!"

"Mrs. Marble, please!" Dr. Orion tried to rein her in.

–"Nefertiti's got some lip on her!"

"Case of the missing muchacho. A mother's license. Like the gentleman said, we're all in this together," Belfry allowed, "any clue to the lad's whereabouts?"

–"Believe me, you'll be the last to know!"

"Please excuse her. You know how women get!" Dr. Orion smiled condescendingly, hedging his bet, ready to jettison his companion at any moment should she prove a liability. "Honestly, my dear," he scolded her like a schoolchild, "you might have a little respect for the Law. These gentlemen are just doing their job." Being a seasoned intimidator himself, he was easily intimidated and eager to please. "Archeology has always fascinated me," he grinned through his teeth. "I mean, the sooner we dig up and obliterate the past the better off we'll be," he added, lest there be any misunderstanding. "What is history, after all, but a compost heap of human

PETER WORTSMAN

error! Thank goodness, we know better now!"

"Bravo! Bravo!" Agent Belfry applauded. "That was quite a little lecture! And who might you be?"

–"I am, Sir, Dr. Cliff Orion, Central Indoctrination Director, Block 367790, and if I may, a serious contender for Block Inspector!"

"Inspect this!" Quirt raised his eliminator.

"Down boy!" Belfry reined in his rash partner.

"I never liked school," Quirt sulked.

"Let's not run through your academic record, shall we!" Belfry cut him short. "Now then, Mr.... Mr..."

–"*Dr.* Orion, like the constellation!"

"He looks more like the Milky Way to me!" Quirt snickered.

"Now then, Doctor," Belfry took control of the interrogation, "what brings you and your lady friend to this particular destruction site at this time?"

–"We're looking for her boy."

–"Been looking hard?"

"Very hard!" the principal grinned and winked. "Isn't that right, Mrs. Marble?"

She grinned and winked back, and a wave of suggestive cramps sent him flying to the floor, with both hands clasping his middle.

"Indigestion," Mrs. Marble shrugged. "I told you not to have that live eel sashimi for lunch, Doctor!" And turning back to the ever more impatient agents: "The principal collects educational artifacts. You didn't happen to turn up a pencil sharpener, a paddle or a dunce cap in your digging?"

"Things would go better for you and the boy if you cooperated, Ma'am," Belfry urged with a practiced sincerity.

But Mrs. Marble didn't bite: "Wouldn't want to spoil the fun of the chase for you gentlemen."

"As you like," Belfry blinked. "We're wasting precious time and oxygen."

His partner, meanwhile, peered with rapt interest at the writhing pedagogue: "First time I ever seen a principal punished," Quirt grinned.

"*Saw* a principal punished!" Belfry corrected.

3.

"It's not that we don't believe you, son," Yosemite said, "it's just that no one's ever seen a bird in flight. People have dreamed of birds, of course. Wuppertal included an imaginary hummingbird perched on the only fruit-bearing branch of an otherwise barren tree in his depiction of the after-paradise. His hummingbird, however, has an unmistakably human expression."

"But what if it really was a bird and came from elsewhere?" Elgin refused to concede. "That would mean that there *is* a way in and out! Isn't there a story like that in some old document file?"

"There is indeed," the old man nodded, "Noah and the Flood, only his was the inverse of our condition. Selected to be the sole human survivor, along with his wife and children, of a deluge which he predicted would drown mankind as a punishment for their iniquity, Noah built himself a boat and took his family and two of every living species along with him aboard. His neighbors thought he was a harmless old lunatic and paid him no mind till they were washed away in the rising waters. So Noah floated around with his little menagerie for 40 days. And when the waters began to level out, he sent a raven and a dove to search for dry land. But the birds soon returned. Then seven days later, he sent the dove out again. And this time, it returned with an olive leaf in its beak. He waited another seven days and sent the dove out again. Only this time it did not return. Nice story!"

"But what if it really was a bird and came from the outside?" Elgin refused to concede.

Yosemite smiled sadly: "Would it still have one head and two wings, I wonder? Or would it be some mutant monstrosity? A two-headed eagle with claws genetically engineered to rip through steel, a heat-sensitive beak designed to ferret out its prey in bunkers, and a single wing that made it flap and fly in savage curlicues!"

The old man lay a calming hand on the boy's shoulder, which the latter promptly shook off in a fury and leapt up from the table.—"What kind of Crabs are you? Afraid to find the way out? Or are you just dragging your feet, digging your own grave?"

4.

After the interminable time he'd spent in a tiny cell, Wuppertal was more at home with rock than people, though he liked the sound of children, dogs, water and wind in the tunnels, as it distracted him from his otherwise suffocating solitude, teasing it into an almost pleasant tingle. A tall man with white hair, ice blue eyes, massive hands and a stoop, the very idea that he might ever stand up straight made others dizzy.

Elgin spotted him now from afar caressing the bare wall in an as yet unadorned corner of the caverns. Well aware and a bit embarrassed at having happened on a private scene, the boy watched as the man passed his hand across the rough contour, now cooing, now cursing, now kissing, now slapping the stone with the open palm of his right hand. Beside him were buckets of paint of his own fabrication, as well as tools of every description, including a hand drill, a hammer and a chisel. First with his face, crushing his nose and mouth, then stretching like a shadow in search of a body, Wuppertal pressed his entire length, from head to toe, against the bare rock, as if he meant to meld with it, to do what people do in private when no one else is looking. Elgin felt a strange disturbance in his breast: his heart thumped as he watched Wuppertal tremble. And it seemed as if the rock trembled too, softening somehow to his touch, and while never ceasing to be inanimate, met his humanity halfway. And the man, in turn, while never ceasing to be human, seemed to take on the stiffness of stone. And covered with dust from head to toe, he looked like a misshapen stalagmite.

The boy kept perfectly still in his hiding place behind a rock and might have escaped the man's attention, but a cry surprised them both from behind another bolder.

Wuppertal lowered his stony gaze, his fury melting into a smile as a petrified Equator poked her head out from behind the rock. "You've brought a guest," he said.

"He brought himself!" the girl protested, not sure if she was being thanked for a gift or chided for having broken an unspoken rule.

Elgin rose up out of hiding now like a foolish afterthought. Feeling all the more embarrassed at having been watched watching Wuppertal, and by Equator of all people, all he could do was shrug.

"A kindred grain of sand!" the old man nodded, his jaw twisting into the semblance of a grin. "How is it back in the upper bulb of the hourglass?"

They all spoke in riddles. Struck dumb, Elgin stared at the talking statue.

"Bedrock!" Wuppertal beat his chest, as if in answer to an unasked question. "You can carve it into blocks, stack it into pyramids and skyscrapers, and pretend you have the upper hand, but it's still rock. Men like Pygmalion, Praxiteles, Michelangelo and Rodin tried to tame marble and impose a human shape, as if stone's sole purpose were to comply with human expectations. Now it rock's turn. Mankind is nothing but a bunch of strutting statues, imitating imitations!"

None of this made much sense to Elgin or Equator, who kept exchanging looks of anger and complicity, each blaming the other for getting him or her into trouble, and yet grateful for having a partner in crime.

"About the bird!?" Elgin finally blurted out.

–"What bird?"

–"The bird of paradise in your mural—is it real?"

"Is it *real?*" Wuppertal parroted the question with a sarcastic grin that ran diagonally like a crack down the middle of his face. "He wants to know if the bird is real. He thinks maybe I've got a bird in my brain, that this egg shelters a bird brain!" Wuppertal slapped his skull hard with the palm of his hand and cooed. And grabbing Elgin by the shoulder, he bent down to bring his parched lips up close to his ear: "It's real alright! As real as me or you, or the girl or the wall—and like us all, it came from dust and will return to dust!"

"But did you see it or just imagine it?" Elgin demanded.

Wupperthal stared a moment. "Saw it, I imagine," he smirked. And picking up a paintbrush, he turned back to the rock.

The visit was over.

5.

"What do you think of the caveman?" Equator teased.

"What is it with you people anyway?" Elgin burst out, feeling the first trickle of all the pent-up anger of his 16 years, and liking it. "Can't anyone ever give a straight answer to a simple question?"

"Uh-oh, looks like our little Vertical's got an ax to

grind!" Equator liked to see how far she could push before the mask of politeness cracked.

"Answer the question!" Elgin insisted.

They were playing a game of will and neither was willing to give in.

"We Crabs react obliquely, sidestepping attacks, in case you haven't noticed." She illustrated her words with a sidelong dance step.

"That's cowardice and denial!" he accused.

"That's survival, son!" she countered.

It was her superior tone and the ever-present smile on her lips flitting between disdain and amusement that finally made him snap. Before he knew what he was doing he had lashed out with the palm of his hand, but there was no sound to the deflected slap, and the hand, at first immobilized then released and redirected by skillful fingers that gently guided it from her cheeks to her breasts, gladly let itself be led. Elgin liked to recall what happened next and replay it in the delicious slow motion of memory. Spectator and participant in an arena of interlocked limbs, he relished above all else that moment when, whipped to a froth and channeled through a portable pipeline, anger boiled and bubbled over into a distilled essence, and all of the carefully inculcated vertical virtues of childhood dissolved before either had time to undress.

PETER WORTSMAN

"Better luck next time!" she laughed.

Stunned and disappointed at his clumsiness, and more than a little bit ashamed, Elgin looked up.

Equator chuckled: "Don't look now, but we're being immortalized!"

Wuppertal had been watching them all the while. It didn't seem to bother her one bit.

–"Isn't anything private here?!"

–"Didn't we watch him?"

–"That's different!"

–"If it weren't for Wuppertal, Yosemite says we'd remember nothing. His eyes, he says, are our Orient Express."

–"What's that?"

–"A fabled train with big picture windows and plush seats to lean back and watch the world fly by."

–"Pretty picture for people going nowhere!"

–"On the contrary, Yosemite says we're moving faster than the speed of memory. Wuppertal's our engineer and conductor, lighting and calling out each station stop. Someday, says Yosemite, we'll pick up enough speed to break through, and then he'll tell us where we are."

–"You really believe that?!"

Hesitating, Equator let a hint of doubt escape from behind her swagger.

"Listen," said Elgin, "I'm beginning to think your caves are not so very different from our towers after all, just another version of our lock-up laid out flat. You want to know what else I think? I think you Crabs keep digging out of habit, just to keep busy and kill time. I think you've forgotten why."

"I think you think too much!"—She laughed and leapt to her feet.

–"Wait!"

But before he could say another word she was gone.

Wuppertal was gone too.

On the wall of the cave where he'd been standing, Elgin found a painting of two butterflies fluttering around a black flower, their wings entwined with the petals, and a bird with a hungering human eye hovering close. The paint was still fresh. Elgin reached out with the back of his hand to wipe away the image but managed only to catch and cut his knuckles on the stone beak, reopening the scratch and adding a few drops of blood to the bird's indelible pigment.

6.

Park fingered the trinkets he had retrieved from his last foray, while mentally formulating his report. The presence of the objects helped, as they made tangible the fact of his having gone away and come back. The crinkle of the clear plastic front of a box excited his index finger. Pressing down hard and breaking through, he felt the contour of a votive figurine he'd picked up at the site of an archaic crash, what the IVT labeled "the consequence of free horizontal license." Two once mobile conveyances turned sarcophagi, with mummies miming life.

He dwelt a while on the shoes, a little black pair that must surely have belonged to a child, and a red pair with sharp pointed toes and heels that narrowed to the diameter of an icicle. The votive figurine in the plastic box wore a similar plastic pair in pink. Her tiny feet were tilted downwards. Surely such shoes were not meant for walking, but only for ceremonial appearances. Certain archaic cultures, he had heard, bound women's feet to cripple them and keep them from running away. Was this votive figurine with its protruding plastic breasts and frozen smile the idol of such a cult? He looked over the box for some clue, but all inscriptions had faded or been worn away, all except for the big bold curling letters: B A R B... A primitive fertility fetish, more than likely, Park concluded, for those desperate 21st-century women who tried to force conception beyond menopause before the policy of birth restriction put an end to such barbaric practices.

He decided to bring Meadow the figurine for a

lark, that and the little shoes, as a reminder.

He wanted a child. She was dead set against it. "I'm a diver, not a breeding machine! I like the foreplay," she liked to joke, "it's the messy aftermath I dread." She'd been so doggedly anti-maternal that it surprised (and pleased) him to see how quickly she'd taken to Elgin. He, too, felt a great fondness for the boy—which made the prospect of betrayal doubly difficult.

*

As soon as Park reentered their domestic circle, Meadow kissed him on the lips while fingering his sack of loot. It was their little ritual.

"My my, but Daddy's been good to me!" she cooed, holding up the treasures. The red icicle-heeled objects made her laugh. "What ever were they for?"

"Walking," said Park.

Meadow tried them on and strode around the circle, taking great pains to keep her balance, before letting herself fall into Park's arms. "More like torture instruments," she mused.

"To keep women from running around," Park quipped.

"Pretty!" she remarked, turning the votive figurine about, moaning in sarcastic ecstasy as she stroked every curve and incline with an inquisitive finger. "Plastic women don't get pregnant."

Park grabbed the figurine from her hand and smashed it, head-first, against the stone wall. The head fell off and rolled away, its face peering up with an insipid smile, which Meadow now mimicked as she bent down and reinserted head in torso.

–"Daddy didn't mean it, babydoll!"

Park grabbed her by the arm, fury fueling passion.

This too was a regular part of their ritual.

Only then did he notice the boy huddled in a corner.

"He's got to learn sometime!" Meadow grinned.

"Yosemite's waiting for my report," Park muttered, storming off, angry for reasons he could not admit, turning over in his mind various versions of the truth.

VIII

1.

Inter-Eye News Bulletin: "The search goes on for Elgin Marble, the boy abducted from Block 367790, who, as of downtime today, is still reported missing. Authorities suspect an unsavory derelict from Block 367789 as the likely kidnapper. The suspect, spotted by block police loitering in an out-of-service freight elevator, is described as a Caucasian male of medium height and build, weighing approximately 168 pounds, last seen wearing a green acrylic jumpsuit and a gray jerkin. Individuals with any clues as to the boy's or the suspect's whereabouts are strongly encouraged to contact the police immediately. The suspect may be dangerous.

"We take you now to IVT Headquarters, where the officers on the case, Agents Belfry and Quirt, have called a press conference, detailing a possible linkage between the boy's abductors and a terrorist threat."

Reporter: "Could you tell us what we're up against here? Is there a link to organized Crab activities?"

Agent Belfry: "We haven't ruled out the possibility of Crab involvement. A King Crab was spotted at downtime day before yesterday scurrying around an archeological dig, where traces of the boy's presence have been found. Unfortunately, the suspect made a desperate run for it and authorities were forced to neutralize his destructive capacity before debriefing him."

Agent Quirt: "He had a nasty pair of pincers, he did, till we boiled him pink!"

Reporter: "Could you tell our viewers how to identify a Crab?"

Agent Belfry: "That's a tough one, I'm afraid. It's a common schoolboy's myth that Crabs are ugly creatures with distorted features and pronounced horizontal tendencies. That, alas, is a fallacy. The common Crab looks much like you or I. He walks upright with manly bearing. Chances are you've passed a Crab in the corridor or rubbed shoulders in the commuter elevator without ever suspecting it."

Reporter: "What danger do they pose to our society?"

Agent Belfry: "Crabs will stop at nothing to sabotage our vertical values. Whenever an elevator cable snaps, you can be sure the Crabs had a hand in it. Life as we know it is of little concern to them and they are even inclined to sacrifice their own to achieve their nefarious ends."

Reporter: "But where do they get their resources?"

Agent Belfry: "A very good question. To fund their activities, they deal in contraband artifacts stolen from archeological digs. The problem is, the demand for these obsolete trinkets continues to grow. People don't realize that in paying for a seemingly innocuous little knickknack from the past they are supporting terrorism. Children seduced into smuggling think it a lark, a thrill, a chance to flirt with the forbidden and make a little pocket money."

Reporter: "Is smuggling a possible link to the kidnapping?"

Agent Belfry: "We believe so. The lad from Block 367790 was an amateur trader, a 'hobby robber,' as we call them, but before he knew it he was in over his head, a good boy gone bad. The Crabs had him in their clutches."

Announcer: "So there you have it. We'll keep you updated on this breaking story. Stay tuned and stand tall!"

Sponsor: "And now a word from Biobright! Ever dream of modifying your genetic makeup? Want to improve your looks? Beef up your IQ? Don't let a faulty chromosome stand in the way of your happiness and success! Now with Biobright's unique new patented genetic alteration process, you're just a marrow transfusion away from perfection! Remember, trust Biobright today for a bio-bright tomorrow!"

2.

–"What's eating you, Orion?"

   –"Nothing."

   –"Fess up!"

   –"Well, if you must know, madam, I'm…irregular."

Ellen let out a laugh: "Is that all?"

   –"I feel as though my gut were riddled with thumb tacks."

The pill was doing the trick. A minor side effect. She decided not to press the issue. Shining her torchlight in all directions, she could not get over the vastness of the space around her, never having seen anything quite like it. Accustomed as she was to narrow corridors and cramped cubicles, the expanse of actual unencumbered, uninhabited area made her dizzy and a bit uneasy. It was as if an intangible guardrail or safety net, as if an invisible buffer had suddenly dropped away from the heretofore constricted boundaries of being and that she might at any moment either take flight or tumble into the bottomless abyss.

"They'll be watching us now!" she muttered aloud, turning in search of invisible eyes. But the fear of being spotted was strangely comforting, as it made her feel a little less alone.

Orion shoved the spectacles back over the bridge of his nose and straightened his back, mindful of his public persona. He spoke with his P.A. system voice, his words intended for invisible microphones: "As respectable citizens aiding the IVT in their search, we have nothing to fear!"

Ellen replied, likewise for public consumption: "What makes you think I'm going to help you find him?"

"On the contrary," Orion sought to assure his position and win additional points in the inevitable future interrogation by clearly attempting to wear down her resistance, "our cooperation can make all the difference! Rest assured, Mrs. Marble, they'll find him sooner or later, with or without our help. They always do. But the sooner they find him the better things will go for him…and *you*. Who knows what corrupt notions the Crabs are injecting into his mind at this very moment, and what acts he is being forced to engage in? Let's hope it's not too late! If he were *my* son, and I do feel a certain undeniable concern for the poor wayward lad, why I'd do everything in my power to save him from their clutches!" Having publicly disavowed any illicit compliance and proved his vertical virtues for the record, enveloped by the darkness, he could not help but eye Mrs. Marble up and down, recalling once again the scene in his private cube. "I do, of course, appreciate your position!" he winked.

"ORION, YOU'RE A SWINE!" She shouted loud enough for the microphones to pick up the sound and the sentiment.

With which the echoing underground dome thunderously concurred: "ORION, YOU'RE A SWINE!...ORION, YOU'RE A SWINE!"

3.

Park knocked two ceremonial stones together at the threshold of Yosemite's domestic circle.

"Welcome back!" the old man smiled. "The community is always concerned during your extended absences, you in the tunnels and Meadow in the rivers. I wish you both were involved in some less risky business, or at least in it together. Ever think of going back to teaching?"

Park shrugged: "Philosophy is hardly an essential skill."

–"Oh, but you're quite wrong, our young people need flexible minds more than you realize: psychic survival demands a subtle grasp of paradox."

"The contradictions of freedom in an enclosed cavern are clearly self-evident! The young know it better than we do, just watch them play hide and seek. But I didn't come here to engage in sophistries, Yosemite," Park concluded testily, "I came to deliver my report."

The old man lay a comforting hand on the younger man's shoulder: "What's bothering you, my friend? Is it the stress of your assignments? You and Meadow ought to take a good long downtime stroll or a swim."

–"I get plenty of walking and she gets plenty of swimming done."

–"We're all in this together, Park. Please let me help."

–"Thanks, but the only worry on my mind right now is the security of this settlement!"

"Insecurity," the old man replied, "is a given we've all learned to live with. But we do appreciate your efforts to keep us safe. What's new up there? Their elevators are still running, I trust!"

Park cracked a wry smile: "Nobody'd think of taking the stairs, if that's what you mean." The smile dissolved suddenly: "IVT is after the boy. It's only a matter of time."

"I'm sure they could save face with an old docu-segment of a simulated rescue," Yosemite shrugged, "and then follow up with a touching feature story on the target's astounding rehabilitation as a proper upright citizen."

"Not this time," Park shook his head, "IVT wants a public lesson."

–"And Elgin's to be the sacrificial lamb?"

–"I'm afraid so."

Yosemite took a deep breath and let out a long heavy sigh: "They'll be after us then?"

–"They already are."

–"What do you counsel?"

–"It's not up to me, Yosemite, it's up to the entire settlement. A roundtable at downtime."

–"What do we tell the boy?"

"The truth." Park turned to leave, then glancing back over his shoulder. "Or a lie, if you like. We'll make it a lesson in paradox."

4.

Nimble as a lizard, Equator easily and altogether unexpectedly broke through a thin barrier of earthy resistance in the pit of a new hole dug into the recesses of the rock just off the southwest tip of the main tunnel, when a powerful wind came rushing through, covering her with dirt and dust and sweeping her back in its thunderous wake. She was the precious *needle* of her digging detail, the advance person charged with priming each recess, gauging density, tapping for minimal resistance.

Most digs were uneventful. An exercise in getting

dirty.

But this time her companions, the Crabs she'd grown up with, had to drag her out by a rope attached to her ankle. Elgin, who'd tagged along, knelt down over her, prepared to give mouth-to-mouth resuscitation, when she opened her eyes and puckered her lips, flashing him a cocky grin. "Go ahead, Prince Charming!" but with all eyes upon him he turned away in shame, the butt of a hearty burst of collective laughter.

Having crawled toward the opening she'd made, the headman, also known as the *nose*, sniffed about: "Smells more like an earth-shattering fart!"

This time Elgin joined in the laughter.

Every digging detail comprised a *needle* and a *nose* and ten *pincers* to do the digging. It was a plodding, grueling, thankless task at which all Crabs took turns, a compulsory spell of drudgery with no payoff at the end of a shift but sore hands and a heap of dirt. But an unspoken faith fueled each thrust of the pick and shovel, a collective longing drove the drill bit deeper and deeper. And though openings in the rock often proved nothing more than calcified pockets of trapped underground gas, every grunt was accompanied with a silent prayer that this time they'd break through at last.

Equator and her detail spent the rest of the shift enlarging the opening. Unaccustomed to pacing himself, at his turn Elgin almost immediately tired himself out digging and had to stay behind, feeling useless, while the others pressed on. As the *needle*, it was Equator's privilege and risk, once the gap had been sufficiently enlarged, to be the first to crawl through.

She flashed her torch, first to the floor, where she planted her hands, then to the walls, reading the word *Lincoln*, inscribed in grimy white—a name she remembered from backtime lessons, the man who'd freed the slaves and landed a bullet in his brain by way of thanks—and then she turned the torch to the ceiling of the great gap that swelled out into a cone overhead. "It's an un-collapsed tunnel to somewhere!" she shouted, to which the others replied with a cheer. For a tunnel meant miles of new corridor to add to the claustrophobic settlement, conceivably a link to other Crab encampments. "I'm going on ahead!" Equator called through the hole. It was a perilous honor that no one could deny her.

"I'm coming with you!" Elgin called back. The others exchanged knowing winks as he climbed in and elbowed his way forward.

Equator caught hold of his hands and yanked him out the other end of the hole and slapped him on the bottom: "Is my baby alright?"

Belly down in the dust, Elgin slowly raised his head and gasped at the great tiled tube of roadway with a faded yellow line running down the middle.

5.

The downtime meal completed, Yosemite directed the ritual recital and called the gathering to order: "Our friend Park has something to say."

Park got right to the point: "IVT wants the boy." He paused to swallow a glob of sputum caught at the back of his throat. "We must consider our options."

It was the first Meadow had heard of the matter and she gaped at Park as if a stranger had infiltrated his soul and annexed his face. Was this the man with whom she had shared all the private rituals and intimacies of the domestic circle?—"You can't be serious, Park! What's there to consider?"

Even Field was taken aback: "Am I to believe my ears? Has our high-minded protector finally seen the light?"

Unable to look Meadow in the eye, Park glowered at Field: "Not the light, but the darkness at the end of the tunnel!"

"There's nothing to consider!" Meadow cried out, her voice trembling with a volatile mix of emotions. "We've welcomed the boy into our midst, he's one of us now!"

Yosemite raised his hands to silence the murmur of agreement. "Park merely recommended that we consider our options. Common sense demands that we do so with a clear mind, and," he added, turning to Meadow, "an open heart. Let us say, for argument sake, that we withhold the boy. The détente we've achieved over decades would instantly be compromised. You don't really believe they couldn't—and wouldn't—put their entire security apparatus on our trail and root us out, if they so decided! Flooding the tunnels with sewage or poison gas would do the trick, or simply sucking out the oxygen. The fact is, my friends, our existence, tenuous as it is, serves their ends. For without us Crabs, there'd be nothing to combat, no threat, no mortal enemy, no magnet for their malaise. Now let's say we handed the boy over, as distasteful as the prospect may be, what do you think would happen to him and to us? They might go hard on him, but then again they might opt for leniency. And even if they chose to hold him up as an example, wouldn't it be in their best interest to demonstrate their ability to rehabilitate a converted Crab, to neutralize any lingering horizontal tendencies and remold him into a model upright citizen? And as far as our survival is concerned, they'd blow up a tunnel or two, filming the collapse, thunder on a bit about the peril of the intractable Crabs, and soon enough go back to business as usual. Why, my friends? Because they need us to contrast virtue and vice and bolster the founding principles of their vertical world!"

Now it was Meadow's turn to interrupt the murmur of approval: "Haven't you all forgotten something! The reason the first Crabs dug underground to begin with, and why we go on digging! Freedom's a concept, not a commodity! If we hand over the boy, we might just as well blow it all up and bow in obedience to the IVT." She glared from face to face, reserving her darkest scowl for Park, who winced, tried and failed to flash a smile to hide it.

A terrible silence hung in the cavern air, a silence that cut through the easy camaraderie of downtime like a knife, leaving permanent scars and sharp gashes in longstanding bonds of friendship and love; a suffocating silence that might have banished speech and loving embrace and encrusted the Crab world with bitter resentment and recrimination, had it not been suddenly broken by the whistling and lighthearted laughter of a weary but jubilant digging detail late to return, all eyes fixed on Elgin and Equator, hand in hand, leading the way. The antithetical moods, the noisy merriment of the diggers and the morose silence of the roundtable, clashed like eggshells breaking on bare rock.

"Sorry we forgot to knock!" Equator tested a grin, only now noticing the tension. "Good news," she reported, holding onto her joy like a precious possession, "we hit pay dirt, tapped a hollow vein, an un-collapsed tunnel with miles of black-top, and maybe just maybe, a way out."

The report was greeted by silence.

"That's terrific!" Yosemite responded with a marked lack of enthusiasm.

"What is it with you Crabs?" Elgin challenged. "It's time for celebration and you mope like you're at an occupant disposal ceremony!"

Whereupon all eyes turned to him.

The joy drained from Equator's lips. "It's about Elgin, isn't it?"

Yosemite nodded.

–"They're after him."

He nodded again.

–"And you intend to hand him over!"

"The decision," he said, straining to keep his voice steady, "has not yet been made."

Elgin listened intently, but with a strange detachment, as if the individual of whom they spoke were someone else, someone he knew very well, an old friend whose absence he would surely miss, though he would no doubt get over it in time. And indeed, there was some truth to this self-deception, for he had said goodbye to that boy, and though still languishing in his gawky hand-me-down body, a chrysalis of uncertainty, he already felt the boy's skin exploding around him and the man about to leap out. Then, little by little, it dawned on him: It's me they're talking about. And taking in all the disparate looks of concern, sympathy, guilt, pity, betrayal, and worst of all, obliviousness, eyes peering right through him as if he were already gone, he responded with an awkward grin.

"You can't!" Equator screamed.

"We're all concerned," Yosemite tried to console her. "We'll weigh our options and decide what's best for him and for us."

"Vertical hypocrites!" she shrieked.

Meadow took the weeping girl into her arms, casting a venomous look at Park, who turned away. "Come along!" she motioned to the bewildered boy.

6.

Inter-Eye Bulletin: "According to an as yet unconfirmed report from a reliable source, authorities are working on a new lead as to the whereabouts of the kidnapped boy from Block 367790. The IVT cautions, however, that when and if they do find him, given the ordeal he's been through, the boy's physical and psychological condition are likely to be unstable. He will surely be remitted to a wellness facility for reconditioning and debriefing before returning to normal life. This is Igloo Domain reporting...

And now a word from our resident psycho-regulator, Dr. Alcove Campanile, on the psycho-quirk of the week.—Doc!"

–"Thanks, Iggy! If you've ever been at a loss for words, you may be suffering from aposiopesis, a clinical condition characterized by a sudden and dramatic disruption of a thought in the middle of a sentence. Until recently, there was little that could be done to correct this condition. In certain rare cases, stricken individuals fall into an extended silence, sometimes lasting days, weeks, months, and even years, and sometimes never snapping out of it. Now there's a cure. Psycho-regulators call it an oral resuscitator, in common parlance, a cattle prong. It's a tiny electrical device the size and shape of a marble slipped under the patient's tongue that literally shocks him back on the ball. This is Dr. Alcove Campanile. Stay tuned and stand tall!"

7.

Sifting through the rubble of the destruction dig at Grand Central Station in search of clues to Elgin's likely whereabouts, the principal and the boy's mother both happened to look up simultaneously at the frozen face of the great clock, that impassive dictator of time that once ruled the lives of hordes of horizontal commuters, mercilessly regulating their coming and going; and though its arms stood still at the 12th hour—uptime or downtime, take your pick—it still radiated a hypnotic illusion of control from which it was difficult to break free. Pondering the lives of the poor wage slaves of the 21st century and the force of progress that made such insect-like swarming obsolete, Dr. Orion smiled with unabashed vertical pride, Mrs. Marble bit her lip. And turning to face each other in wordless disaccord, both fathomed in a flash that the effect of the suggestive implosion pill she'd slipped him would be wearing off any minute now and that the balance of power between them would once again shift. The realization of this imminent change gave rise to a flurry of unspoken calculations, as of two chess players devising new strategies.

What surprised the principal most, though he never would have let on to it, was that he did not necessarily anticipate with pleasure his release from her control. Quite the contrary, the power she held over him these last…23 hours, 53 minutes, and 47 seconds, to be exact, had stimulated the tendrils of his long-stunted emotions, rousing such attenuated sentiments as attachment, camaraderie and even tenderness, not to speak of a tingling in his netherparts. A lesser man might have called it love.

She, for her part, felt nothing but loathing for him, a loathing tempered by a mounting terror at the cognizance of her imminent loss of control, and of his hand in her son's and her own fate, camou-flaged by a smile.

Each, of course, did his or her best to hide any overt signs of the changing power relationship, though the beads of sweat on Dr. Orion's brow and a tendency on Mrs. Marble's part to suck and bite her bottom lip belied the mask of calm. Yet neither admitted to any discomfort.

"It's a toss-up," Dr. Orion shook his head. "The boy could have taken any track, and who's to say he ever did make contact with the Crabs!"

"You mean to say he could be lying out there un-conscious in the dark…or…" Mrs. Marble did not dare complete the thought.

"I'm not saying it's necessarily so, only that it might be," he said, testing out a certain guarded newfound sensitivity to her suffering. "Chances are he was indeed picked up by a Crab scout and taken to one of their encampments. They're always look-ing for new recruits. In olden times, a ragamuffin band of horizontal wanderers called Gypsies were said to have swelled their ranks with kidnapped con-scripts: an extra pair of hands, though rumor had it, they sometimes cut off a finger or even a foot, as a cripple made a more pitiful and productive beggar."

Mrs. Marble winced.

Sympathy notwithstanding, he still enjoyed turn-ing a thorn in an open wound, and did so, despite himself, to begin to reassert control.

–"Shut up, Orion!"

–"So sorry, my dear."

"We're just turning around in circles," she said.

"There are more than 30 tracks on this level alone," he objected, "who knows where they lead."

Mrs. Marble stopped suddenly at the gate to Track 21. "Wait a minute!" she whispered, hearing a sound as of something rhythmically rubbing against the rails.

8.

Park spotted the man and the woman at the mouth of the tunnel long before they saw him. Under ordinary circumstances, he would have thought twice about making contact, but a sense of urgency forced him to take the risk.

"How kind of you folks to have come to pick me up at the station!" he called out cavalierly as he hopped from the handcar to the platform and bounded up the stairs to the gate.

The man gave him a sour distrustful look. The woman smiled.

"We've been waiting for quite a while!" she responded in kind, feeling greatly relieved at the presence of a third person, particularly a man, to dilute the intensity of Dr. Orion's hold on her.

Orion was disappointed for precisely the same reason.

"I'm afraid I missed the express!" Park grinned back at the woman, deciding for the moment to ignore the man.

"You're not IVT then!" Dr. Orion deduced.

–"*They* took the express!"

"We'd invite you for a cup of coffee, but the coffee shop is under renovation." Mrs. Marble motioned to a dangling café sign, enjoying the repartee.

The principal had had enough: "Where's the boy?"

"Didn't notice any other passengers!" Park peered behind him down the empty platform.

Orion snarled: "Cut the crap, Mister!"

–"Not very polite, your...er, husband, Ma'am!"

"He's *not* my husband!" Mrs. Marble shuddered at the very idea, which made her turn suddenly serious. "You don't look very menacing for a Crab."

"I wouldn't jump to any rash conclusions, Ma'am!" Park objected, in part to maintain the flirtatious undercurrent of their communication, but also because of a kindred confidence which he immediately felt in her and an instant distrust in the man.

–"I'm the boy's mother!"

–"Elgin's Mom?"

Her face flushed with emotion at the sound of her son's name. "Then he's alright!?"

"Fit as a freight!" Park assured her with a wink at Orion. "Who's the heavy?"

–"A not so innocent bystander!"

Dr. Orion shoved the spectacles back over the oily bridge of his nose. "We're wasting time. Where's the boy?"

Park held a finger to his lips: "We can't talk here."

*

Squatting in the dark nearby, tapping his earphone, Agent Belfry hissed: "Did you get that, Quirt?"

–"Sorry, Sir, I was just wedging a wad o' wax out o' my right ear."

IX

1.

From the lull in the constant hum of conversation and the darted looks, Wuppertal could tell the passersby were upset about something. "Let them choke on it, for all I care!" he muttered to himself, mixing his pigments, passing the palm of his hand over the rough rock surface he was about to embellish. He had more sympathy for a bulging stalagmite longing to couple with a fetching stalactite than for the foolish conundrums of his own species. But something was different this time. Even the little ones were audibly upset. The timbre of their shouting was thin and muffled, the pitch strangely subdued. Their yowl and yap had no bite to it. This bothered Wuppertal, not so much because he really cared about their well-being, but because he needed to feed on their vitality to nurture the faint echo of humanity still left in himself. Without the children's chatter to cheer him or even to curse at when it got too loud he was little more than a lump of lifeless matter, a carbon deposit in suspended animation. There had been times during his long incarceration on the 13th Floor when the thump of his heart was the only reminder that he was still alive.

He'd once felt so lonesome he befriended a fly that somehow managed to get in. Fed it. Tried to teach it tricks. Let it land on him where it pleased, scurry down naked limbs, himself refrained from bathing in the basin provided, for the fly's sake, letting it languish in sweaty dipterous erogenous zones. It was an ordinary red-headed housefly, nothing exotic. But he liked to watch it rub its hind legs gleefully and turn in a frenzy. On one occasion while admiring its wild St. Vitus dance he noticed with an adrenal rush that its tail was the same color as its head. He shed a tear when it died and composed a ditty:

The stone alone my throne,

The treachery of tears.

The head is but a bone,

A hollow bowl of fears.

Singing it again and again, he would break out in fits of laughter that invariably ended in weeping, but at least he knew he was alive.

When things got really bad, he was hard pressed to keep from dashing his skull against the rock. And when the sadness passed, he sank into a trance of ever increasing duration.

*

Equator shook him.

"Damn!" he muttered, pleased despite himself at the disturbance.

–"They're thinking of sending him back!"

–"They can damn well send anybody to hell or

the 13th Floor, for all I care!"

–"IVT is after him."

–"That's one less Crab to feed."

–"They're undecided, but I'm afraid the cowards will give in!"

–"They always do."

–"Please, Wuppertal, I know you're not as heartless as you pretend to be!"

He looked surprised, for he had never knowingly pretended to be anyone or anything other than who he was, but the girl's words found a crack in his unacknowledged shell.—"What do you want, child?"

–"I want you to help!"

He shook his head, recalling their last little run-in that inspired the private symbolism of an obscure section of his mural.—"You two seem perfectly able to help yourselves!"

–"Please, Wuppertal, help us escape!"

–"Tunneling's not my trade!"

"I know you can do it," she insisted, "you taught us as children how to play boulders and pebbles."

–"That was just a game!"

"Please," she said, "you know what they'll do to him."

He peered at her.

–"Please!"

He'd watched her grow from a child into a girl, and lately noticed a new fullness to her figure.

She flashed him a look well aware of her flowering allure and its affect on him. "I'll model for you, I'll do anything you want."

Wuppertal pictured the pleasure then wiped the slate clean. Much as he might have relished it, the prospect of physical proximity repelled him. "Mad girl!" he snarled.

2.

"They'll be waiting to welcome you home!" Park cautioned.

"Of course," Mrs. Marble concurred, "I hadn't thought of that."

"The school's the safest place!" Dr. Orion insisted.

"He's right," Park nodded, "can he be trusted?"

–"Not as far as you can spit!"

*

The principal punched in the code and his office door slid open. "Do make yourselves at home," he said, "I'll see to coffee."

Once he had left the room, Mrs. Marble turned

with a sigh of relief to the stranger: "I don't know what he's up to but I have my doubts about the quality of his coffee!"

Park grinned back.

She laughed.

Under the circumstances, the laughter felt both strange and strangely comforting. "Why do you trust *me?*" he asked.

–"I don't have much choice, do I!"

–"There's always a choice."

They gave each other a searching look, uncertain of just what they meant.

–"How's Elgin?"

–"Safe…for the moment."

–"How much longer?"

"I don't know," he said, "there's pressure to deliver."

–"Pressure?"

–"IVT!"

–"I didn't know the two worlds were in touch."

–"We make occasional contact, of necessity."

"Necessity," she smiled again, "the frantic mother of invention…I wonder what's keeping him."

"Brew's ready!" Orion came bustling back in, tray in hand. "My simulated secretary's on the blink. I had to make it myself. Cream or sugar?"

–"Black."

"The same," said Mrs. Marble.

Orion poured, adding a dash and a spoonful to his own cup. "Life's a bitter pill. I prefer the illusion of sweetness."

Mrs. Marble took a gulp. "I'll take that sugar after all!"

A buzz at the door drained the color from her cheeks.

"Dear me," said Dr. Orion, "did I forget to tell you there'd be a few more guests?"

Whereupon, at the press of a button, the door slid open.

Agents Belfry and Quirt crowded the threshold.

"So good of you to make it," Orion nodded. "I believe you know everyone here."

"It's Mata Hari and Benedict Arnold!" Belfry grinned.

Park nodded, averting Mrs. Marble's stunned expression.

Altogether lacking his partner's poise and aplomb, Quirt squirmed: "I don't like bein' in no principal's office! Takes me back to the trials and troublations of childhood!"

"That's *tribulations*, Quirt," Belfry corrected, "at

which, I'm afraid, this dear lady is just getting started."

3.

Spreading a fleece over the sleeping boy, hesitating
between a motherly protectiveness and the desire to
put him out of his misery, Meadow contemplated
smothering him in his sleep. Life is precious, she
decided, however long it lasts, and planted a kiss on
his forehead.

Tossing and turning, already on the run, eluding the dream police, Elgin kicked the blanket off as
soon as it fell upon him and sat bolt upright, watching Meadow don her second skin for diving detail.

Turning, she laughed at the intensity of his gaze.
"Better save it for Equator!"

–"Where is she?"

–"She'll be back."

–"Where are *you* going?"

"Listen, Elgin!" She knelt down beside him. "I
have never been a very good liar. Your arrival stirred
up a can of worms.—To think that the man I once
trusted the most..." she couldn't bring herself to
finish the thought. "Field may well turn out to be
the most honest of us all. Ugh, they disgust me, the
whole crawling lot of them. I don't belong here any-

more. I'm leaving the same way I came."

His worried look belied all the childish fear he tried desperately to hide.

"There's only one air tank," she shook her head. "Let's hope the new tunnel Equator found leads somewhere."

4.

Yosemite considered how best to execute the will of the council. He could not face the boy himself.

Field sidled up behind him: "The sage can't soil his hands, I understand. Didn't know surgeons were squeamish."

–"Spare us the sarcasm! It was the will of the majority."

–"And *we* concurred."

–"To invite collective retribution would be reckless endangerment. I have to consider the good of all. You remember what happened to the Crabs that harbored a run-away in the Midtown Tunnel!"

–"The rumors were never confirmed."

–"No, but the bloated bodies that washed up on our embankment—don't tell me they were just out for a swim!"

"How and where do they want him delivered?"

Field got down to business.

–"Alive at Gate 2. Chloroform might make things a little less messy. You can use Park's handcart."

–"Speak of the devil, where is friend Park?"

"On another mission, I imagine," Yosemite shrugged and turned his back. As soon as the sound of Field's snickers and footsteps receded, the old man doubled over, heaving in disgust at the smell his own deceit.

5.

"Meadow's gone," Elgin told Equator, trying hard to save face. "It's funny, you know, losing two mothers in a matter of days."

"No time for nostalgia," the girl shrugged, more grownup than her years, "they'll be coming for us soon."

–"*Us?*"

"You didn't think I'd let you have all the fun!" she grinned. "We'll have to send them on a wild goose chase to give us enough time to escape!"

6.

The Nose complained of stomach trouble and did

his best to stall for time, dragging his feet, dropping the drill, so that another member of the detail had to be dispatched for a spare drill bit. Field egged them on with taunts and threats, but they were none too keen to ferret out the whereabouts of their precious Needle. Shovels were broken, chisels bent, curses hissed. "I could have done better digging by myself!" Field fumed. It took them the span of an entire shift before finally managing to enlarge the hole enough for Field to fit through, and then they refused to follow, pleading fatigue.

Field wasted no time arguing, but set off on the run, finding the shreds of tires and an occasional shoe, but no trace of the fugitives. He kept on running at a steady clip, until, out of breath, his advance was blocked by a seemingly endless double-lane back-up of rusted boxes on wheels. In each one patient skeletons, some with surviving patches of skin and hair, sat behind a wheel, waiting. The thin dry air of the tunnel had preserved their poses and even, in some cases, their facial expressions. One gazed at itself in an overhead mirror with the mummified hint of a smile. Another with its mouth open held out an outstretched middle finger. A third had its bony digits folded behind its skull in seeming repose. There were couples entwined, and entire families in suspended animation, adults up front, children in the back seat, frozen in transit. Rats had gnawed away at all appendages, including ring fingers around the indigestible metal, and toes, where the leather was soft enough to chew through.

Feeling sick at the sight and dizzy for lack of oxygen, and knowing he ought to turn back now, Field yawned and shone his torchlight on the wall. A faded sign warned: ENTERING NEW JERSEY. With his last conscious thought, he wondered what sort of place it was and why people were dying to get there.

7.

What troubled Park now, glancing at the woman, was not the guilt of betrayal (a feeling he had long since learned to live with) but the strange tug of attachment between them that survived a shared consciousness of his apparent deception. Naturally there was the erotic element, a woman is a woman, stress makes the adrenalin and other hormone levels rise; but there was something else, the realization that, come what may, they were in this together.

–"Used to be a teacher, isn't that right?"

"Come again?" Park perked up, suddenly aware of the tail end of a remark directed at him.

"I *said*," Dr. Orion stressed with a pedagogue's evident impatience, "I understand you used to be a teacher."

"That's right," Park nodded.

"Ain't we a comfy company!" chuckled Quirt, making himself comfortable on a settee. "Two chalk talkers, two flatfoots and a retired tart!"

"What made you leave the profession?" Orion inquired.

"I don't know," shrugged Park, "too many questions, not enough answers."

"That's my problem!" Quirt chimed in.

"Among others!" Agent Belfry could not resist the dig. "Now then, Mrs. Marble, we have a few questions we'd like to ask you. Mere formalities, you understand, pending the boy's imminent apprehension. Preparations for his personality profile, at which our friend, Dr. Orion here, will officiate, and you, dear lady, will watch through a one-way mirror."

Mrs. Marble stared at the floor.

"Give her a break, she's had a long day," Park objected.

Quirt sniggered: "'N she's got a long night ahead!"

Whereupon the unthinking fingers of Park's right hand balled into a fist and the fist collided with Quirt's jawbone, which slacked and dropped open; an elbow met Orion in the solar plexus; a knee bunted Belfry in the groin; while the left hand reached out and grabbed Mrs. Marble's right and dragged her out the door. No one was more astonished by this round of rash acts than Park, who now found himself running down a corridor with the woman in tow.

8.

It was Wuppertal's expression, the cryptic look in his eyes when he said it that made Elgin uneasy. "What do you mean, enter the rock?"

Equator had tried to explain it to him as best she could, though she herself didn't really understand. She had never actually seen it done, nor had anyone else in the colony, but the desperate circumstance, the fact that he was being tracked down at that very moment by her own people, and when captured, would certainly be returned to suffer a fate she preferred not to imagine, drowned out any doubts. "It's a kind of about-face, an inversion of self and other," she parroted the words of the elders. "Fossils are the petrified cusps of life embedded in rock. Wuppertal just speeds up the process."

"Makes perfect environmental sense," Elgin nodded, "but I find it a little hard to identify with a dinosaur egg!"

Whereupon Wuppertal actually cracked a smile, an occurrence so unusual for him that it split the parched brittle skin around his eyes and lips, the sting of which made him wince. "There's still time to back out."

"And do what?" Equator asked, "serve himself up on a dissection palette to the IVT? They mean to make a lesson of him!"

"Alright," Elgin conceded, "I'm a vertical lesson in tough love, but *you* don't need to do this!"

"You didn't *need* to come here!" Equator snapped.

Such a somber, stone-like look reasserted itself on what passed for a face, that it was hard to imagine the old man's eyes and lips as anything but cracks. "The process," he warned, "is irreversible."

"But you yourself are living proof that it works!" Equator challenged.

–"I'm an accident, and who's to say I'm all here, or that I didn't leave the better part of me behind?"

The three of them looked at each other long and hard.

Elgin broke the silence: "Let's give eternity a try!"

Wuppertal tapped and rubbed the rock, alternately nodding and shaking his head. "Now," said the old man, his body hard up against the selected surface, turning round as if in a sudden fit of rage. "Pretend I'm not here and do what you did that other time!"

"No way!" Elgin protested.

But already her hands were in motion, one stroking him, one guiding his fumbling fingers. Her eyes were upon him too, and the combined effect of touch and sight distracted him, soon enough neutralizing shame, creating a screen of sensation as they shed their second skins.

His unskilled hands set off on a journey of exploration up desert dunes and down dry gullies, slipping on a sudden mudslide to where the wetness promised a well of sweet water.

To hell with Wuppertal! To hell with the IVT! To hell with Crabs and Verticals! To hell with everyone and everything but here and now! he thought, grabbing handfuls of hair and inhaling its fragrance. Equator went momentarily limp. And in that instant Elgin shed the last hesitation of boyhood.

He was man and she was woman and there was nothing else but desire and rock!

And all the while, neck twisted, Wuppertal watched, muttering curses and endearments, begging and prodding the wall to give way, until he felt the first tremors, as of an earthquake, and knew the boy and the girl felt it too, for he was in her now and both their hips were heaving. And Wuppertal reached out and grabbed them, and pressed them hard against the rock, himself upon them, a sandwich of flesh, so hard he could hear their bones crack.

One last spasm and it was over and done with

and the bodies of the boy and the girl slumped forward and fell to the ground, drained of their essence.

Wuppertal kissed the wall and wept.

X

1.

Inter-Eye News Flash: "Family and friends of young Elgin Marble, the boy from Block 367790 abducted by Crabs, can heave a sigh of relief. The boy was found early uptime today by archeologists digging in a restricted destruction site far beneath the zone of habitation. How he got there remains a mystery. Doctors report he is in a coma and suffering from severe physical trauma thought to be the result of a crash. The prognosis for the boy's recovery is guardedly optimistic. He has been remanded to a wellness facility, where a complete physical examination and personality profile will be conducted as soon as his health status permits. In a bizarre twist to this incident, the boy's mother, Mrs. Ellen Marble, a former horizon parlor hostess, likewise from Block 367790, has been reported missing. Stay tuned and stand tall! …Ladies, have you ever wondered what it's like to change your face? Now with Will-Me-Beautiful!, a patented new hybrid psycho-dermo modification device, it's as easy as changing your hair and eye color. You'll like the way you look! You'll like the way he looks at you!…

2.

"They've found him!" cried Gladys, eyes glued to the

Inter-Eye screen.

"Found who?" Herbert, Sr. muttered over breakfast.

–"Elgin!"

"Ready for disposal, I imagine. Pass the toast!" he said, unenthused.

–"But now *she's* missing!"

–"Who?"

–"Ellen!"

"Good riddance, I say!" he munched.

–"You're a heartless man, Herbert!"

"Say, Gladys," he perked up, "what about their cube?"

–"What about it?"

"Well," he wiped his mouth, "with Upton out of the way, Elgin out of commission, so to speak, and Ellen missing, the space *is* vacant."

–"What ever are you driving at?"

"A shame," Herbert shrugged, "to let it gather dust! It does, after all, abut our cube!"

A half-smile curled at the left corner of her lips, while the right was busy mourning.

–"With my connections and your pull as IVT floor chairlady, we might, how should I put it, pluck a few cables in our favor!"

The smile now reached from ear to ear.—"Oh, Herbert, you're so…so…very vertical!"

"Good uptime!" Herbert, Sr. reached for his briefcase. "Up and at 'em, that's my motto. Get ahead or get out of the way!"

"Still I do hope they go easy on Elgin!" Gladys fretted.

"Look where easiness got him!" Herbert, Sr. scowled.

"I suppose you're right, dear. Your father's off to the office!" Gladys informed their offspring.

Herbert, Jr. blinked goodbye.

"'At a boy!" Herbert, Sr. grinned, giving his son a feigned right hook to the jaw.

To which the boy responded with a stoic double-blink.

3.

Institute for Vertical Thinking, Psychosocial Division, Anti-Intransigence Section Document Number 93387304200.79

Classification: CODE 13

Description: Electro-record of the Personality Profile of Elgin Marble, age 16, resident of Block

367790, 59th Floor, currently committed until further notice to Block Wellness Ward 000069.

Examiner: Cliff Orion, Ph.D., principal of Central School, Block 367790

Q: Hello, Elgin.

A: [No response]

Q: I do hope this isn't going to be a one-way conversation.

A: [No response]

Q: You're here for an IVT-prescribed personality profile. You do understand that your cooperation is imperative, and that should you continue to remain silent, I will be forced to stimulate response with jolts of electric shock of ever-greater intensity.

A: [No response]

Q: Now let's begin. Is your name Elgin Marble? Answer yes or no.

A: [No response]

Q: I will now administer a low-level shock.

A: [No response]

Q: I'll take that as a yes. How old are you, Elgin?

A: [No response]

Q: You're sixteen, aren't you?

A: [No response]

Q: I will now administer an elevated shock.

A: [No response]

Q: For simplicity sake, I will express my expert opinion, to which you are free to assent or object, as you see fit. Now then, Elgin, certain personality traits, notably a pronounced internal tilt, latent horizontality, and a stubborn intransigence, all left unchecked by your irresponsible parents, have resulted in behavior of elevating gravity, including truancy, trespass on off-limits destruction sites and illegal trade in contraband artifacts, and finally, cavorting with unsavory elements in the cracks and crevices of vertical society commonly known as Crabs. Stop me if you have any objection, wish to offer a clarification or qualification.

A: [No response]

Q: Let it be noted for the record that the subject has produced no objection, clarification or qualification of the reasons for the alleged behavior. Said conduct has endangered, not only the subject's own physical and mental condition, as illustrated by his failure to respond, but also, by example, imperiled the physical and mental condition of his schoolmates who might be tempted to follow his lead. Isn't that right, Elgin?

A: [No response]

Q: Now then, considering the subject's reckless conduct and the corrupting influence it would surely have, both on himself and others, if left unchecked, implicitly suggesting that such extra-vertical behavior were countenanced within the purview of harmless pranks, and furthermore, considering the subject's intransigence in the face of repeated warning, and his obstinate refusal to cooperate with these proceedings prescribed for his betterment, for his own good and that of society, this examiner duly recommends a protracted course of compulsory desensitization. Does the subject wish to respond?

A: [No response]

Q: I will now administer a high-level shock.

A: [No response]

Q: We will take that as an affirmation of the facts of the case. Let Elgin Marble be remitted for desensitization to Block 367790 Wellness Ward, located on the 13th Floor. Does the subject have anything further to say?

A: [No response]

Q: So be it. Let the recommendations be preserved for the record and promptly implemented.

4.

Following the initial elation and rush of satisfaction and relief at the close of a case, Agent Belfry invariably suffered a protracted bout of emptiness in the face of the void.

Quirt's needs were more mundane: "Wada ya say we hop an up to a ho-ho?"

–"Speak English, Quirt!"

–"Sorry, Belfry, I forgot, you ain't conversant in the block lingo."

–"Why is it that I never seem to suffer from my apparent cultural and linguistic deficiency, except in your company?"

The irony was lost on Quirt, who smiled sympathetically. "I was just suggesting we hop an express elevator to a cozy little horizon parlor for a rub down."

–"No point going home to an empty cubicle, what!"

–"There's a hot new pit with simulated tunnels and Crab beds up on 369½. I hear the hostesses speak French."

–"English will do, thank you. Lead the way, old man!"

"Speaking of hostesses," Quirt inquired on the way up, "what ever happened to Beauty and the Beast?"

–"Libido under stress and whatnot. They belong to science now."

–"Did they let 'em go then?"

"With an electro-leash to monitor their comings

and goings," Belfry chuckled.

The elevator door slid open at the desired location.

"It's Old Spectacles!" cried Quirt, recognizing Dr. Orion at the threshold of the Seventh Heaven Horizon Parlor.

Orion turned, aghast. "What a…surprise!"

"Why if it ain't *DR. O-RION, CENTRAL SCHOOL PRINCIPAL!*" Quirt took pleasure in loudly declaiming his name and title and watching him squirm. "Why who'd 'a thought a man of your breeding was a patron of such a place!"

"Official fieldwork!" Orion countered defensively.

"Nothing wrong with a little horizontal lapse every now and then, keeps you upright, eh!" Belfry smiled.

Quirt elbowed Orion in the ribs. "It's like our own little school reunion. Pity you couldn't bring your girlfriend, she was quite a number!"

–"Quite!"

–"But then again you still have the lad to diddle with," Quirt goaded him on. "A little pedant-nasty on the side, it's a principal's purgative!"

"That's *pederasty* and *prerogative*, Quirt!" And turning to Dr. Orion, Belfry shrugged: "A hopeless case of pedagogical failure!"

Orion was speechless.

"So what'll it be, Bag-cock and the Sin Cities tour?" Quirt chortled. "Or a little cruise of the penile colonies?"

"Your errors are precious, old boy!" Belfry chuckled. "I'm almost inclined to concede that a proper education would only have spoiled your natural wit. Wouldn't you agree, Dr. Orion?"

Orion nodded nervously: "Undoubtedly!"

"Will we be enjoying the pleasure of your predatory company then?" Quirt flashed a crescent full of silver-capped teeth.

"Actually, I was j...j...just leaving!" stammered Dr. Orion, a forefinger trapping his slipping spectacles, and scampered off like a frightened rat.

"Pity," said Belfry, "we would have learned a lot!"

5.

—"That's funny!"

—"What?"

The fugitives had collapsed out of breath on a broken bench in the shambles of a cordoned off corner in the pit of Grand Central Station.

"The clock," Mrs. Marble remarked, "its hands are frozen at 12. A station in which time stands still.

No arrivals. No departures. Wouldn't it be wonderful if time really could stand still and the world just went on turning!"

"Life is action!" Park objected.

A rustling sound disrupted the silence.

"What's that?" she started.

–"The rats, I suppose, impatient for their dinner!"

Mrs. Marble winced: "You sound almost sympathetic!"

"More than that," he said, "I'm envious. Nobody bothers to keep tabs on them. They have the free run of the place."

Both the man and the woman felt a profound weariness. They'd been running down endless corridors, riding innumerable freight elevators, dodging into doorways, eluding real or imagined pursuers. Both felt, without saying so, that they'd come to the end of the line. And there was a certain relief in this realization.

–"Haven't heard any footsteps in a while. Think they've given up looking for us?"

–"Fat chance!"

–"But what if they have?!"

"In that case," he smiled, "I'd have to turn us in."

–"You're joking!"

–"Yes and no."

Mrs. Marble was stupefied: "What was the point of helping me escape?"

Park shrugged: "I don't know."

Mrs. Marble laughed out loud, casting caution to the wind: "I'm in love with a lunatic!"

Park wrapped his arm around her: "That makes two of us!"

Again they heard the rustling of rats.

–"They're hungry."

–"We're the leftovers!"

–"Elgin, you, me, the rats, we're all part of the same social experiment, aren't we!"

–"I suppose so, yes."

"What'll it be, breast or thigh?" she smiled, lay back on the bench and pulled him toward her.

6.

Flippers kicking, arms outstretched, Meadow was in her element.

Reading her gauge, she realized that her oxygen tank was near empty, but this didn't bother her much, she who had always felt on land like a desperate seal stranded on the rocks. Better to drown clean than to rot high and dry. Perhaps human life on land had been a mistake, after all, an error among many that would be rectified now or in a millennium or two, when another deluge would reclaim the swarming homonoids and wash the earth clean of their foul encrustation. And this time there would be no ark to save any specimens of the mutant breed—all this Meadow mused, swimming through the channeled tide down under the great eastern landfill, hoping this time to reach whatever was left of the open sea, rejoicing in the fact that her lifeless body would keep bobbing forever like an Anich ball to China and back.

7.

There is a myth that locked in the rock around us are the spirits of two lovers forever joined, and that when the earth quakes it is their hips heaving. One day, it is said, the rock will split open, civilization as we know it will crumble from its foundation to its lofty tip, and all life will be engulfed in a jet of molten cum, the lava hardening into a bed of stone. And on that bed the lovers will lie. And she will give birth to twins, a boy and a girl encased in rock until the time is right for them to break out like birds from the shell. And from the bedrock will erupt a tall blue-green emanation, part tower, part tree, sprouting branches and piercing the sky, with a naked couple looking up from the topmost branch and a child waving down from the clouds. And so it will all begin again from the beginning. Only this time things will be different.

Lexicon of IVT Approved Acronyms and Sayings

AI	Anti-intransigence
EB	Elevator bandit
EN	Electronic notification
EO	Elevator operator
For up's sake!	For heaven's sake!
HP	Horizon parlor
IE	Inter-Eye
IO	Internally Overactive
IVT	Institute for Vertical Thinking
ODC	Occupant Disposal Chute
PP	Personality profile